Advance Praise for *The Pa*

"Readers will enjoy … adventures after she finds … of her new foster home, but it … pens her heart and learns that people … omplex than they appear that she finally fin … he place she belongs. Vivid imagery is woven into this beautiful story about discovering connections in unexpected places."

~ Miriam Spitzer Franklin, author of *Extraordinary*

"I'm in awe of the talent of the author and how she has created this realistic but also magical world woven them together in so much care and vivid detail. She's just genius."

~ Joey Susan, Goodreads reviewer

by
Rebecca Weber

Illustrated by
Sarah Ann Doughty

ISBN: 9781951122461 (paperback) / 9781951122553 (ebook)
LCCN: 2022941805

Printed in the United States of America.

Kinkajou Press
9 Mockingbird Hill Rd
Tijeras, New Mexico 87059
info@kinkajoupress.com
www.kinkajoupress.com

Content Notice:
This story includes scenes that involve foster care, children running away, adults yelling at children, and of being trapped in a burning building that may be traumatic for some readers. The story also includes thunderstorms, dogs, cats, and one mischievous leprechaun.

Table of Contents

This book is a love letter to my amazing sister, Sarah, who is without a doubt the most incredible artist I know.

It's also dedicated to my dear friend Elli, who believed in the butterfly before it found its wings.

And to my Aunt Corinna Elizabeth Emily Kurth-Baker, whose luminescent soul always deserved to fly.

"I feel that there is nothing more truly artistic than to love people."

~Vincent Van Gogh~

Chapter One

Moonlight

On any other night, the glowing sheen of ivory moonlight against shiny hardwood floors would have been a pretty sight to behold. But as Nova crouched close to the ground and carefully maneuvered her bedroom door shut, blood pounded in her ears at the stark vulnerability of this eerie light. The group home sat stock still, as if waiting for her to make a mistake and alert the caretakers to her escape plan. She held her breath and listened beyond the ruckus of her heart. The entire facility hung suspended in a far-off dreamland. Not even the flutter of moth wings puttered against the nearby windowpane. Maybe she'd be able to pull this off after all.

Shouldering her backpack and steeling her resolve, she lowered her belly to the floor and crept down the corridor, inching like a sneaky caterpillar to the back stairs... the ones that lead to the kitchen. The front foyer would be a stupid move, with the manager's office ablaze in light, even at this hour. Nova could picture the manager tilted back in her wooden rocking chair, facing the office entrance should any of the foster kids wake from a nightmare and need a cool glass of water. Even in sleep, the woman was diligent. So, Nova would have to exit through the backyard. A cold sweat dripped down the curve of her neck as she scuffled toward the shadowy staircase, fingertips scratching against the fibrous wood floor. Freedom rang in her ears like a beautiful ballad. "Nova," it sang. "Go home." But home had never been anything more than a gamble, a game she always lost. She was ready to play her only hand.

Gently, she tackled the staircase, one creaky step after another. She tiptoed along the edges of the boards, shifting her weight to keep the house's groans minimal. Nova had thrown her hair into a ponytail to keep it out of her face, but the hairdo pulled at the corners of her forehead, and she grimaced, wishing desperately to free her locks. Soon.

At the bottom of the stairs, Nova peeked around the corner to investigate the empty kitchen. The normal bustle of children and staff had vanished, like someone had taken an eraser to the scene and scrubbed out the people. She allowed herself a small intake of air as she ogled the back door. Nova knew the manager liked to make hourly rounds to check on the children. A clock above the stove ticked to urge her on. Tensing her shoulders, she sprang into action.

Hopping expertly to the back door, Nova unlatched the chain and twisted the deadlock with a feverish click, squeezing her hands against the doorknob to gather the last of her nerves. Softly, she coaxed the door open, praying under her breath this decision was the right one.

A small cough echoed behind her, and she froze. Twisting her head to the side, Nova spotted a tiny silhouette lurking in the opposite door frame: one of the youngest foster boys in red fire truck pajamas, thumb stuffed in his mouth and unruly black hair contorted into weird shapes. Nova raised a trembling finger to her lips and made eye contact with the boy. "Please," she begged him telepathically. "Don't tell." He didn't move. She took her brief chance, slinking out the door and into the darkness beyond.

She hurried around the side of the group home, gripping her backpack to keep her hands from shaking. Was she really going to do this? Nova had a hunch where she belonged, but the journey would not be easy. And even when she arrived, she'd have to fight for her place. But maybe that's the point of a bet. If you win, the prize is worth it. And what did she have to lose?

But Nova didn't even make it to the driveway. Fate doesn't always cooperate. A strong hand caught her by the arm and a familiar voice whispered in her ear. "It's always the quiet ones." The manager waggled a disapproving finger close to her nose and clung to Nova's shoulders, guiding her dutifully back into the group home. The pale moon cried above them, tears of shimmering moondrops speckled along the pavement, a reflection of Nova's resounding disappointment. She pondered struggling for a moment, pushing the woman to the side and bolting down the driveway, to the street. Deep in her heart, Nova knew she wouldn't get far. Ripping her hair tie from her head, she shook out her tresses and released the tension in her muscles.

Maybe not today, maybe not tomorrow, but soon. Home is where the heart is, and Nova's heart knew one reality: nomad.

Chapter Two

A Long Road

Her new transfer began well before dawn, so early the birds were still dozing in their nests, and the stars twinkled lightly in the sky. Nova blinked, groggy, when they shook her awake. She untangled herself from the mussed covers. Then, robotically ran a comb through her shoulder-length brown hair. She rubbed the sleep from her leaf green eyes and grabbed her few belongings with practiced hands, draping her favorite sweatshirt over her shoulder. Chilly morning air blasted her face when she exited the group home. Nova shrugged on her sweatshirt and zipped it up all the way to her chin. The manager and caretakers each took turns giving her a hug, but she knew it was more a formality than anything.

Once she'd said her paltry goodbyes, Mr. Briar, her hefty companion in the gray suit jacket, made a show of opening the trunk of his car as if Nova actually had anything to stow in the back. She shook her head at him, casting her eyes toward the ground and clutching her denim backpack more tightly. Mr. Briar shut the trunk with a quick snap. He straightened his faded tie and ushered Nova into the car, muttering about beating the traffic and sticking to the schedule. The coolness of the leather seats seeped through her jeans, adding to the jarring morning chill. Glancing at the reflection of the group home in the rearview mirror, numbness vibrated through her entire being. Goodbyes are meaningless when you have nothing to miss. Nova fastened her seatbelt decidedly as the car shuddered to life and resigned herself to the dim view outside the front windshield, her fate in Mr. Briar's clumsy hands.

Nova was used to being uncomfortable. So many days and nights spent in temporary places left her feeling akin to a dandelion seed caught up by the wind. It drifted from forest to mountain to field, settling only for a moment, before the breeze carried it onward and away. This life of constant motion was exhausting and relentless. But the routine was good for one thing—never having to look back.

How would it feel to put down roots: to attend school, do household chores, and make lifelong friends? To stride through the door at the end of a rough day into a warm, authentic hug? The visage of a beloved young girl with blonde tresses appeared in her mind's eye. Nova shoved the memory away as tears sprung to the corners of her vision.

The thoughts bled into one another as the scenery changed. Blacktop transformed to gravel, and the new road lent a rugged bumpiness to the journey. Fields stretched as far as the eye could see: rows and rows of seedling corn stalks and leafy beans. Nova leaned her forehead against the cold glass of the window, reflections of the rural landscape swimming in her eyes. The hours and miles flew by.

A barren field sparked wayward memories of broken promises. A massive tractor ripped open the nearby field with its powerful rototillers, and Nova winced as the sharp blades of loss pivoted simultaneously in her gut. Faint images of all the times people had abandoned her broke her mind's surface and bogged down her spirit. It was the happy places Nova refused to revisit in her recollections. She hid the lost contentment away in the furthest part of her subconscious. Sometimes, she would dream of the good homes and the people who had burned a hole in her heart, especially the blonde girl she locked up tight. She had learned the hard way in her twelve years of life that nothing could last forever.

Some seeds never get the chance to grow. Inevitably, no matter the previous destination, she always ended up back in this car. The exterior of the vehicle was black, full of dings and dents much like her mood. The mirror up front hung at a lopsided angle, studying her like it was trying to read her thoughts. She frowned in its direction and was met with two brown, unsympathetic eyes staring back.

"Nearly there," Mr. Briar mumbled. "According to the directions, anyway." He gazed offhandedly at a paper copy of the route marked with scribbles, arrows, and the like. Evidence of how the datedness of the car was a direct connection to its owner. Nova crossed her arms and harrumphed. He had tried unsuccessfully to enter the address into his ancient phone before they started their trip. The paper copy was his back-up plan.

The air conditioning in the car had given out long ago, and the lack thereof transformed the space into a makeshift sauna, morning chill long banished by afternoon sun. Nova yanked off her sweatshirt and balled it up in a lame attempt to combat the heat. Sweat brimmed on Mr. Briar's forehead and dripped onto the collar of his worn suit coat. Yet he refused to remove the jacket. Nova had to give him credit at least for that. He was professional to a tee.

Nova was bored enough to flip through the magazine Mr. Briar had tossed to the back seat for her. It was full of fashion tips, quizzes to find out if he really does like you, and inane advice columns. None of the readers had ever written in to ask: "How do I find a place to belong?" Useless trash. She judged the length of the trip by the number of times Mr. Briar fiddled with his tie, a habit repeated every ten minutes. Nova lost count somewhere near thirty.

That's when the good ol' clunker read Mr. Briar the riot act. The dashboard lit up with an angry gas symbol. They had to go left to refill. She practically jumped with joy when they came to the fork in the road, her muscles aching in anticipation of exiting the car. The buildings looked very out of place amidst the endless crops. A small gas station and restaurant sat tucked back from the gravel.

"May as well get something to eat while we're at it," Mr. Briar suggested to Nova. She shrugged non-committal, rolled up the window, and unfastened her seatbelt. She stretched her sore muscles and hurried to escape the stifling confines of the car.

Nova shielded her eyes from the afternoon sun. She had visited many places in her short life, but never anywhere quite as rural as this hodunk country pitstop. The scene looked as if it had been frozen in time for the last fifty years. The old gas station had two pumps out front and a sky blue awning covering the door. Metallic letters dangling across the top read "Fuel and Co.", except the C was so crooked it suspiciously resembled a wayward horseshoe. She restrained herself from reaching out to pretend to straighten it.

As Nova swung herself around toward the restaurant next door, a sudden, intense hunger plowed through her, and her stomach grumbled noisily. She could have drooled at the delicious smell of cinnamon and hot maple syrup lingering in her nostrils. While the gas station looked like it had been neglected for decades, the restaurant was a different story. Though small, the entire building was immaculately maintained. Nova studied the brown brick exterior, eyeing the light pink shutters, pretty flower boxes, and hand-painted sign above the door that read "Ellie's Place" in script. Nova approached a window box and stroked a silky flower petal between her thumb and forefinger. A small chalkboard balanced outside described the specials of the day. Chicken noodle soup, Reuben sandwich, homemade apple pie… the thought of fresh food made Nova salivate and her stomach rumble yet again.

"I'll grab us a seat," she shot back at Mr. Briar as she rushed to the door. He had put on his glasses and was trying to decipher the faded lettering on the gas pump. He waved her onward without turning.

Chapter Three

First Impressions

Nova swiftly opened the white wooden door and a happy silver bell chimed out to say hello. Inside the place was cozy and welcoming, and her head pivoted around like a swivel chair as she took it all in. There were floral upholstered chairs, daisies in vases at each of the tables, and a countertop flanked by pink stools. The establishment was empty but for an elderly couple in the corner, holding hands over cups of coffee adding to the overall wholesomeness. It took all of three seconds to make her selection after snagging a menu, and she planted herself, squirming, on one of the open chairs. By the time Mr. Briar wandered to their table, she was ready to barge into the kitchen and fix her own lunch.

A petite woman in a frilly white apron and a pink cotton dress emerged from the kitchen. Nova peeped over the menu like a spy and made the quick assumption she must be *the* Ellie. With glasses perched precariously on the edge of her button nose and hairnet tamping down her lovely blonde curls, Ellie powered about the restaurant, a woman on a mission to save the world one home-cooked meal at a time. Her smile lit up the room, and the bounce in her step reminded Nova of dancing.

"Hello, Honies," her voice was sunshine, so musical and bright. "What can I getcha?"

"Turkey club for me," Mr. Briar replied. He paused, eyeing Nova sideways as if mulling over the potential damage. She batted her eyes at him. He knew her favorite culinary masterpiece. At last, he relented. "And chocolate chip pancakes for the girl."

Ellie winked in Nova's direction. "Good choice. They're one of the favorites 'round here. Any coffee for you travelers?"

Nova angled him a pleading grin and wiggled her eyebrows. Mr. Briar stood firm. "Just for me."

With that, Ellie swished away to retrieve the coffee pot. In her haste, she abandoned her pencil on their table. It tugged at Nova's fingers like a magnet. Mr. Briar busied himself checking his email, and Nova felt a familiar, unrelenting itch in her right hand, like it was covered by invisible ants. Discreetly, she scooped up the pencil and the itch vanished in an instant. She tucked her hair behind her ears in preparation. Nova pulled a napkin from the holder and positioned herself away from her companion. Her eyes skimmed the room for something worth preserving. She'd been told a while back art was the best way to capture a moment and save it forever, and Nova only drew what she believed deserved to last. She was the judge and the jury of her art... and she sat straight as a pencil when wielding the power of creation. Art was more than a hobby. It was her escape.

When she focused her gaze on the couple in the corner, her hand leapt into motion of its own accord. She tried her best to pay attention to the shadows and how they brought out the details in the scene. Nova's eyes flicked up at the couple and then back to her drawing. Slowly, the napkin transformed into a rough detailed image. Two elderly people were born out of graphite, with hunched shoulders and distinct wrinkles from years of sharing grins. But Nova paid closest attention to their hands. The shading had to be just so to capture the way they fit into one another. The pencil refused to cooperate; every line seemed wrong. Tongue tucked in her cheek like a wad of gum, she tried erasing a few of the features, but the pencil's eraser was practically non-existent. The hands became nothing more than a dirty smudge of gray. Disgusted and scowling, she scrunched the napkin into a ball and pushed it away, the pencil clattering to the table in defeat.

"That's a real talent you have there, Miss," said the light-hearted voice from before. Nova looked up and blushed, nearly snatching the picture to hide it away. She wasn't quick enough. Ellie smoothed out her napkin picture, studying it appraisingly. "The most beautiful creations never come easy. You name it: chocolate chip pancakes, homemade soup, or even my famous apple pie. Took me a good year, a lot of flour, and a burn or two to get the recipe where it is today. But my, oh my, folks come from miles around to get a piece." She laughed, a tinkling giggle that jingled cheerfully like the bell by the front door. Ellie folded the creased napkin gently into quarters and tucked it and the pencil into Nova's hand with fluid grace.

"Best hang on to these. You never know when the picture may want to be finished." Her touch was a whisper of compassion, feather soft, and Nova relaxed her tight, frustrated shoulders. With that Ellie flew away, buzzing around like a bee heading back to the hive, and her spell was broken. Nova slipped the supplies in the pocket of her jeans, and dug into her stack of pancakes, the fluffiest she'd ever devoured, smacking her lips at the incredible sugary goodness of the first bite. There was something to be said for years of practice.

When the pancakes had disappeared and her belly was sufficiently stuffed, Nova glanced over at her companion, still fiddling with his phone. Mr. Briar had moved from his email to the GPS app and was struggling to make sense of the route options featured on the screen. Nova probably could have helped him but instead busied herself studying the patterns of the floor tiles. She traced the lines and angles in her mind. When Ellie came whirling back through, Mr. Briar gave a throaty cough to get her attention.

"I don't suppose you could give us directions," he paused, glancing back down at his phone. "We're looking for 111 Orchard Road."

Furrowing her brow, Ellie's cheerful expression sunk faster than a penny in a wishing well. The reaction lasted only an instant, and she recovered smoothly with a beaming smile. Nova's keen attention latched onto Ellie's hesitation and her belly did a couple of jumping jacks.

"Of course, darlin'," she said, overly cheery. "You'll be heading north to the fork in the road and turn left. Travel along that way for a few miles, and the first right turn you come to, take it. The house'll be on the corner. If you hit the pond, you'll have gone too far."

"Thanks much," Mr. Briar responded, always a man of few words. He fished some cash out of his wallet to pay the bill. Nova sauntered over to the door while she waited, but a bundle of nerves wreaked havoc on her stomach, sending her breakfast for a jittery tumble. The pancakes had been a nice distraction from the real hurdle of the day. She felt her invisible armor creeping back up as she steeled herself for what was to come… a new home, naive hopes, the same inevitable disappointment.

Mr. Briar led the way out the door, fumbling with his keys. Ellie tapped Nova on the shoulder before she could follow. She wore a knowing smile and gave Nova a reassuring pat on the back.

"You're off to the right place, little Miss. I think you'll find that tiny corner of nowhere to be the spot where you belong."

Nova almost snorted in disbelief. She wanted so badly to trust Ms. Ellie, but all she could do was bring herself to shrug and say a hasty "Thanks" before rushing out the door. There had been plenty of people in her past with flowery words and promises which hadn't come to fruition. She wasn't as gullible anymore. There was no way to know for certain what the future held without facing it first. She wished she had a remote control to freeze time until her nausea receded. As sick as she was of grass and fields and no air conditioning, she wasn't in any hurry to acclimate to the house or her new guardian.

About three miles up the road, they reached the turn. The street was aptly named Orchard Road. Blossoming apple trees flanked the gravel, soaking up the summer sun and providing a glimpse of the natural, undeniable beauty of the countryside. The apple trees were lovely to look at: regal, green and welcoming. Their branches dripped with budding flowers and looked like a vision from a dream. If only that dream extended another twenty yards.

At one time, 111 Orchard Road would have made an incredible statement. The three-story farmhouse had intricate details to add character and unique charm. The gables sprouted curved and glorious, and wooden posts on the porch had a hand-carved shape which made them the focal piece of the home. A crooked, discolored brass door knocker decorated the front door. Unfortunately, the rest of the house had seen better days. Faded white exterior paint peeled back on every piece of siding as if the house was shedding its skin. There was a hole in the dark green roof of the garage, large enough it seemed as if a bowling ball had fallen through. The main roof sagged and dipped in a foreboding way that suggested it would soon look the same. The windows were large and dusty, and any interior view of the house was full of shadows. There was no asphalt driveway, only gravel. Weeds were so interspersed through it you couldn't figure out where the driveway ended, and the yard began. Nova gaped and her heart fell into her spastic stomach. Mr. Briar's rearview mirror eyes got wide with shock.

Mr. Briar pulled cautiously off the road to a grassy parking spot and shut off the ignition. His hands gripped the steering wheel a little too tight, knuckles white, and he let out an enormous release of air.

"I'll be needing to inquire with the office about this. The homeowners were cleared through the application process, but I don't see how there could have been an in-person interview," he mumbled under his breath, an edge to his voice.

Nova sat glued to the seat, immobilized with sheer apprehension, her palms sweaty. A headache pounded in her temples. She had been to some neglected homes in the past, but the state of disrepair on this one put them all to shame. She prayed the inside living quarters weren't a mirror image of the outside mess. The care of the house had fallen to ruin, forgotten and abandoned. Nova's eyes stung and she covered her face with her hands. She knew what it felt like to be forgotten.

"Well, let's take a closer look at least. It was a very long trip." Mr. Briar unfastened his seat belt and was out of the car.

Nova hesitated a moment, digging deep into her heart for courage. Like ripping off a bandage, she forcefully grabbed her backpack and exited, trying her darndest not to lunge under the seats like a frightened rabbit. The car creaked as it settled, and she shut the door with an ominous click. Stepping outside was like entering a sauna, the oppressive heat immediately weighed her down. The quiet stillness of the yard broke with feverish barking, and a huge blur of white and gray fur dashed out from under the porch. In that split second, her brain screamed instinctually: 'WOLF'. The animal sprinted straight for Mr. Briar.

Chapter Four

The Sunshine Room

As the blur hurtled toward Mr. Briar, Nova screamed in panic. He blocked his face with his hands, about to be bowled over, when a shrill whistle echoed from the direction of the house. The creature stopped immediately, sat back on its haunches, and turned its head toward the sound. Once it was still, Nova gaped as the gigantic sheepdog shook his shaggy head, its proportions unbelievably large. Its paws were the size of softballs, and its gray and white fur was long and shaggy, covering the animal's eyes making it impossible to read its mood.

Mr. Briar still hid behind his hands; wary the slightest movement might provoke another reaction. Nova tiptoed on eggshells to stand next to her companion, trying to get a better view of the silhouette standing in the front door frame. As the man descended the porch steps, he tied up a plaid bathrobe around his waist, as if he had just risen out of bed. Being that it was the middle of the afternoon, Nova's eyebrows rose a notch in disbelief.

The man walked silently toward them, like a specter gliding into the sun; the light transformed his silhouette into defined characteristics. His caramel brown hair was messy and uncombed. He scratched at stubble on his chin, highlighting his wild and unkempt appearance. An angular nose poked out of his face, and his cheekbones were similarly shaped. His lips were thin and still, set into a straight line and not relaying any emotion. His eyes, however, were a rich deep blue, so captivating Nova was trapped by their gaze. The pupils were alert and attentive, soaking up the scene and not missing a beat.

The man ambled casually but deliberately across the yard, his shoulders stooped ever so slightly, giving his body the shape of a question mark. When he held out his hand in greeting, Nova spied splatters of multicolored paint dried across his fingertips. Mr. Briar hesitated, briefly; before reaching out and shaking the man's hand.

"So sorry about the dog," the man's voice was quiet, almost a whisper, chalky and rough from disuse. "He really is quite harmless." The sheepdog's tail thumped the ground, as if part of an inside joke. Mr. Briar wasn't laughing. Nova itched at the back of her knee with her shoe, averting her eyes from the awkward exchange.

"Mr. James Russell, I presume?" Mr. Briar got back to business, his tone clipped. "We had an appointment scheduled for this afternoon. Did someone from the office call to confirm?"

The man surveyed Nova head to toe, then shifted back to Mr. Briar. "I've been working overtime this week, been out of the house. I may have missed the call."

Mr. Briar continued without delay, patting his briefcase. "Your paperwork was completed sufficiently. I have it right here. But I will need to fulfill a walkthrough to make sure the environment is a... healthy one." Diplomatic with his choice of words. Nova subdued a sarcastic laugh. The house was clearly in disarray.

Mr. Russell was not put out. "By all means, I'd love to take you through. But first, who do we have here?"

Nova kicked a rogue dandelion, sending its seeds into the air with fervor. Mr. Briar cleared his throat as if in code. She tossed him an annoyed glance and straightened her posture.

"I'm Nova." She said matter-of-factly. "Just Nova."

She did not move to shake Mr. Russell's hand, but he didn't seem to mind. He gave her a gentle smile and a nod before abruptly turning to make his way back to the house. The dog followed at his heels, but not before growling at Mr. Briar to remind him of the pecking order. Mr. Briar trailed at a good distance, watching the animal with palpable caution, hands tensed. Nova brought up the rear.

The porch sloped in the center, and the wooden

boards groaned and creaked as they walked across. The doorway was a huge, gaping mouth, so black and dark it could swallow them whole. Nova gulped and gathered her courage, clinging to her backpack as if it were a life preserver on an unknown sea.

Squinting so her eyes adjusted to the dim interior light, she tread carefully through the narrow front hallway of the house. The heavy scent of mustiness hit her straight in the face. Paint cans were strewn about, some empty, some not, obstructing the path and adding to the maze. A doorway to the left of the front hall led to an office. Once Mr. Briar had seen the interior of the room, Mr. Russell pulled the door closed, obstructing the view. To the right of the hall a substantial staircase led up to the second floor. The banister was a twisted knot of warped wood, but oddly inviting. Nova had a random inkling it would be warm if she touched it. A thick layer of dust blanketed everything. She suppressed the urge to sneeze at the tickly flecks disturbed by their shuffling feet.

At the end of the hall was the entrance to a dated, but functional eat-in kitchen, with a small table by a few rear windows, and sparse cabinets lining the wall. Nova's pulse quickened upon noticing a series of padlocks fastened to the back door, and the curtains in the room were nailed down to the window trim. Mr. Briar tugged at them curiously.

"I find the natural light fades the décor," Mr. Russell pointed to the tan plaid wallpaper and a few measly photographs of rural landscapes that decorated the walls. "I paint for my job, so I'd rather not spend my free time doing it here." He laughed jovially to himself, but Nova was unnerved at the sight of the covered windows. The room was claustrophobic as being stuffed in a tin can.

"Shall we continue upstairs?" Mr. Russell prompted.

Heading up the stairs, Nova gripped the banister tightly, the wood worn smooth from many years of use (and just as warm as she had hoped). She realized there must be an attic space, because once they reached the landing the staircase continued upward to the side of them. She craned her neck, attempting to see to the top, but the room was well-hidden. Mr. Russell described the attic pointedly as storage and left it at that.

The second floor was rather underwhelming. A paneled door straight off the landing led to a master bedroom. Further down the hallway were two more doors. The first opened up to a very blue bathroom with cracked tiles covering the walls and the tub. A lacey cobweb resided in the sink, which Mr. Russell brushed away with his hand. All the while, Mr. Briar scribbled messy comments on his notepad.

Across from the bathroom stood the final door. It was a white six-panel door, basic but clean. Mr. Russell reached to open it, and Nova involuntarily tensed, bracing herself for what lay beyond.

"And this... would be your room..." Mr. Russell whispered, looking for all the world like a fish out of water as he nervously pulled at his shirt collar. He dropped his eyes and quickly opened the door.

When it swung ajar, Nova gasped in relieved surprise. The hallway flooded with natural light as she stepped into a wonderful dream. Her eyes drank in the sight like a thirsty traveler lost in the desert, who had finally reached a tropical oasis. The walls were painted the loveliest shade of yellow, and the trim near the floor and ceiling was white and intricate. A sizable canopy bed sat to the right, and a massive white armoire was situated to the left. There was a large window with a cushioned seat positioned directly across from them, allowing an expansive view of the summer sky and the apple orchard beyond.

Next to the bed stood a gorgeous maple end table. The legs were hand carved to be curved and whimsical, and its tabletop was also inspired. The stain captured the grain of the wood like a photograph, pulling every beautiful inch of the material into perfect focus. Dainty flowers and vines had been painted onto the piece, cascading their way up the legs and onto the surface of the table. An antique, stained glass lamp was the bow on top. Nova gravitated to the furniture as if drawn by an invisible string. She walked dreamily through the room, touching each item delicately, worried it may disappear. Her heart radiated warmth, and Nova resolutely decided this room must be crafted of sunshine.

Mr. Briar stood immobile in the doorway, pen poised with a forgotten thought. He too was caught up in the beauty of the space. Mr. Russell seemed particularly withdrawn; he remained in the hallway uncomfortably, as if there was an unseen barrier keeping him out. Nova, beaming from ear to ear, was too enthralled with her surroundings to really wonder why.

After a minute or two of complete silence, Nova still studied each nook and cranny of the room with passionate interest. Mr. Briar asked Mr. Russell to give them a moment to talk. In her peripheral vision, he quickly obliged, rushing back to the stairs like a bird freed from its cage. Mr. Briar shut the door and turned to face Nova. She was sitting on the bed, skimming her hand over the silky comforter, and admiring its softness. His face had grown especially serious.

"From what I've seen of the house, it is livable. The inside, though dated, is not a hazard in any way. And this room in particular seems very well-kept." He paused. "The question remains, though, is whether it's a place you wish to stay. It will only be a couple of weeks until we check up on you again. With the state of the house, I'm going to leave the decision up to you."

He tugged at his tie, loosening it a fraction, while he waited for her reply. A million thoughts pinged around Nova's head like a pinball machine. She cast her eyes once again around the room, and her anxieties softened, appeased by the sweet honey color painted on the walls. It wasn't often she got to choose her own fate. The newness of it made her long for guidance. She wandered over to the window and spied the gravel road in the distance, leading to the horizon and out of sight. Looking at it made her more tired than she could say, and she rubbed her eyes in exhaustion. In that instant, she made up her mind with resounding clarity. She followed Mr. Briar out of her sanctuary to give Mr. Russell the news.

Chapter Five

Blind Exploration

The odd pair stood on the rickety porch, waving goodbye half-heartedly as Mr. Briar's car grumbled back up the road. It kicked up a cloud of dust that was the only sign of activity for miles. Mr. Russell's eyes bore into the back of Nova's head. She willed herself to keep facing forward, feigning interest in a splinter that was dislodging itself from the porch handrail. This was her least favorite part of the process. The get to know you, welcome home speech never quite stuck. Mr. Russell cleared his throat awkwardly.

"So… you've had a long day." He began, hushed. She could hear him shuffling his feet nervously back and forth. "Why don't you go and get unpacked? I'll make something to eat."

That was when she realized he was as ready to escape the conversation as she was. She sideways glanced at him and gave a quick nod, before bolting back into the house and up the stairs. The tightness in her chest dwindled the closer she got to the Sunshine Room. Once inside, she shut the door as a barricade behind her.

The loveliness of the space was just as impressive as before, but now she was able to linger over every last detail. The air smelled of fresh wildflowers, though none were visible in the room. Nova flung herself onto the bed, testing the buoyancy of the mattress. To her great delight, the fluffiness bounced her up in the air. She giggled as she tumbled back into the pillows.

Returning to earth, she spied her denim backpack lying next to the bed. She unzipped it a fraction and checked the inside to ensure everything remained untouched. She pushed a rubber banded wad of cash to the bottom of the bag. She double checked Mr. Briar's paper directions were also inside, having swiped them from the car earlier. Then Nova dug into the pocket of her jeans and withdrew the picture and pencil from the diner. It felt like she'd chowed down on pancakes years ago. Using the pencil, she circled a small pinpoint near the fork labeled BUS STATION, then carefully stored the art supplies in her bag. Glancing at the armoire, she stepped toward it, fully intending to place the backpack inside. She chastised herself immediately, realizing it was too obvious of a hiding place. Instead, she stuffed it deep under the bed, cloaked by the only existent shadows in the room. She had learned in her multitude of prior homes that privacy was a privilege many adults chose to ignore, especially when it came to foster kids. She had taken up the habit of concealing her treasures to preserve a semblance of privacy; the system had served her well in the past. She didn't think Mr. Russell would come looking, with his earlier aversion to her room, but she wasn't going to take any chances.

Trotting over to the window, Nova marveled at the vast, endless fields of crops surrounding the house. Outside of the apple trees across the road, it was like she was on her own rural deserted island. It would make the next couple days all the more challenging.

The armoire opposite the bed was massive, but not imposing. Nova opened both its doors and all the drawers, finding them stocked with clean, well-worn clothes that were the perfect size for a girl of her age and stature. There was also a soft quilt tucked in the bottom, weathered but in great condition. All fifty states were featured on the quilt; it was a colorful patchwork of the country she'd not had the opportunity to travel. She dared to dream that one day soon she would have the chance to visit some of the distant places on the quilt.

The sun started its daily descent, and Nova wanted desperately to scope out the exterior of the house before it got too dark. Heading downstairs carefully, she met Mr. Russell at the entrance to the kitchen. She decided to be straightforward and to the point.

"I'm going outside." She said, feeling stupid. "I

want to look around."

"Of course," was his only reply, his voice crunching like leaves in autumn. It seemed out of practice. Nova could get used to the lack of conversation. Life was so much simpler that way. She had almost made it to the door when another request stopped her in her tracks.

"Take Amigo with you. He's a great tour guide." Mr. Russell chuckled and gestured back into the kitchen.

Amigo turned out to be the sheepdog. Nova eyed him, wary. He was slurping noisily from his water dish. He didn't look like a wolf any longer, but that didn't mean he couldn't bite like one. He trotted over to them once he was finished with his drink.

"I don't know if he likes me very much." She kept a little distance separating her from the dog. He cocked his head quizzically, as if assessing her intentions.

"Oh, he's a big softie." Mr. Russell ruffled Amigo's fur, revealing his previously concealed eyes. The pupils were milky white and completely empty of light. It was then that Nova understood the animal was blind. Some guard dog. She did feel a little sorry for him though.

Mr. Russell noticed her epiphany. He became cryptic.

"He can see more than the average dog, you know. Amigo's got a knack for knowing what a person needs... who they are. And sometimes, like with Mr. Briar, he likes putting on a show. That being said, he's the most loyal dog you'll meet. I guarantee it."

He sounded so sure. Nova held her hand out gingerly to the dog's nose, giving him the chance to sniff her properly. Amigo paused for a moment, as if considering his options, and then planted the sloppiest of all welcome kisses on her hand. The saliva dripped heavily from her fingers to the floor, making an incredible mess. Amigo thumped his tail, proud of himself. Nova felt less sorry for him, and significantly more grossed out.

"All right, then. Let's go," Nova sighed. But the dog hadn't waited for her permission. He led the way with a jaunt in his step, maneuvering the paint cans like he owned the place. He pranced happily out the front door without a care in the world.

Chapter Six

Face First

With dusk came a satisfying relief from the daytime heat. The yard was just as messy as before, with the grass patchy and overgrown in the most random places. The crickets hummed a sleepy tune and Nova could swear she smelled manure drifting from some unseen location. Still, she grew light as a balloon when she got out of the house. The world was bigger, grander, and more approachable in the open air.

She meandered over to the right, passing the open garage, a precarious mess looming within. A rusty blue truck sat in the depths, flanked by mountainous stacks of paint cans. An old ladder rested in the bed of the truck, and beyond that, all manner of practical tools were strewn about, as if a fixer upper tornado had passed through. Hammers, wrenches, saws, and jars of screws littered the space; there were even a few tools she'd never seen before, presumably related to wood as their blades and grooves were covered with a fine sawdust. Nova retreated so as not to affect the balance of the gigantic mess. The last thing she needed was to die in a hardware avalanche.

Looking back at the farmhouse from near the road, she had a good perspective of the porch and its proximity to the window by her room. Just as she'd hoped, the roof was within climbing distance. It wouldn't be difficult for her to shimmy down a corner support post either; Nova had climbed trees with nimble precision since she was young. Her concern rested on whether or not the roof would be stable enough to hold her weight. The sizable hole in the roof of the garage made her seriously doubt it. Regardless, she would have to try. She'd been hatching her plan all day. It was her only real chance to escape.

Amigo had started to growl gently as she pondered her predicament. It was like the dog had a sixth sense on the same wavelength as her brain. She patted his head unconvincingly, trying to settle his nerves.

"There, there... such a good boy."

Perhaps she should walk around a bit, to ease the mood. Amigo tailed her, velcroed to her heels. She made her way over to the side of the garage, and then the back of the house. She picked up the pace to a jog, getting more and more frustrated. With her head turned backward by the sheepdog's follow the leader game, she didn't notice the fence until it collided with her. Nova yelled out in pain, seeing stars, and dropped to the dirt. She rubbed her forehead furiously, glaring up. Amigo stopped a couple of steps back, casting a look at her as if to say, "Who's blind now?"

The fence was immaculately constructed. It had to be at least seven feet tall. The wood was unstained and coarse, like it had been built in a hurry; but the handiwork was commendable. The boards abutted each other so closely a hair could not have fit in between. The fence stretched a long way down the road behind the house and turned right to continue around the backyard. Nova had run into the gate. Thank goodness she'd missed the enormous metal padlock on the latch. That would have been a lump on her noggin. How odd that there were so many locks associated with this backyard... super strange, and a little creepy. Hands on hips, she puzzled over the secured curtains in the kitchen and the latches she had seen fastened on the back door. Any access to the backyard was barred. The dark part of her mind wondered if there were bodies buried beyond the gate. Mr. Russell didn't seem unstable, though he did strike her as someone who favored privacy. She could easily relate.

Dusting off her jeans, Nova took off at a skip around the perimeter of the fence, hoping there would be some kind of gap or hole further down the line. Unfortunately, the woodwork was impeccable. She huffed out a breath as she reached the edge of the fenced yard, hopping lamely in an attempt to see over the top of the wood.

Back here she spied a group of trees standing just inside the border. Huddled together like old friends, their branches, twisted and gnarled, reached high into the sky. Anything below the branches was hidden from view. Nova kicked the fence, frustrated. She succeeded only in hurting her toe. Massaging her foot, Nova caught a flash of brown fur watching her in the treetops. No way. Was that... a monkey? The creature's face was shrouded by leaves, so she couldn't be sure, but she stumbled back in confusion as the furry anomaly vanished into the branches. Heart pounding in her ears, Nova craned her neck for proof of her sanity, but the leaves were solemnly still. Did Mr. Russell have a zoo in his backyard? Maybe her eyes were playing tricks on her.

A serene pond to her left ran parallel outside of the fence. The water was vast and shimmery, expanding the length of a football field just off the property. Tall grasses and cattails rimmed the pond like a frame. The surface resembled a fogged glass and Nova could've sworn if she touched it, it would be solid. Nova whacked at an obnoxious mosquito with her palm.

Amigo followed her patiently around the back of the fence and sat quiet now, much like an unpaid babysitter. A shrill whistling rang out, shattering the silence. Amigo turned on his tail and sprinted for the front of the house. Nova followed carefully, heading around the opposite side of the fence, continuing to look for breaks in the structure. She made it back to the front porch with no such luck.

Mr. Russell stood on the front porch stroking

Amigo's head absentmindedly, staring off into the distance, bewitched by the fields. As Nova approached, his posture straightened, becoming more formal and speaking in almost a business tone.

"Looks like rain..." he trailed off, lost in thought, his eyes as blue as the pond out back. "Oh, and dinner's ready."

He was inside the house before she could reply. She pivoted her head around, searching the sky for even a hint of rain or a solitary cloud, and eventually shrugged off the comment. The storm clouds were as numerous as the gaps in the fence planks. Her instincts told her there was a side to her host that may be a little off-kilter. Nova resolved her will to leave and trudged into the house, mentally ironing out her plan. After all, with no clouds for miles, what could possibly go wrong?

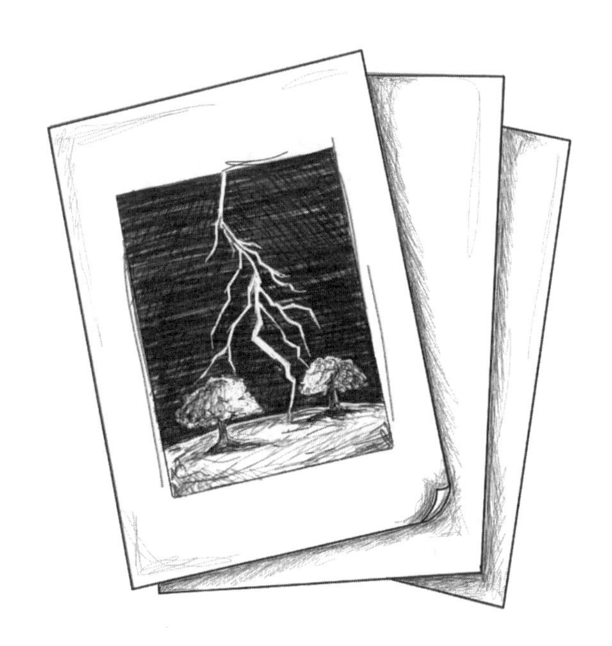

Chapter Seven

The Torrent

After a pathetic dinner of bland soup and blessed silence with Mr. Russell, Nova retreated to the Sunshine Room; the house was quiet and uneventful in the later evening, with only the occasional spider scuttling about in a darkened corner. The sunshine had evaporated, and Nova's room felt like the inside of a pitch-black cave. She lay still on her bed, mentally running through her plan, quadruple checking the steps she'd have to follow. Nova strained to catch any noise from downstairs. She thought she'd heard Mr. Russell climb the staircase over an hour ago, but he didn't attempt to check on her. All the better, as she was trying her darndest to feign sleep, and she wanted to give him ample chance to doze off himself.

Outside, Nova could see the branches of the apple trees swaying back and forth; gusts of wind picked up from earlier in the day. The clouds in the sky were a cold, charcoal gray, looking as if they had been drawn there by pencil. A shocked disbelief rippled through her. The volume of clouds was surprising, and she recalled warily what Mr. Russell had said about rain. She shoved the thought from her mind. A little water never hurt anyone.

Inching off the bed and tiptoeing softly to the door, Nova opened it a crack and peered down the hallway. She expected Mr. Russell's bedroom door to be closed. On the contrary, his bed lay empty, and she noticed a bright flood of light spilling down the staircase from the attic space. That could complicate things. She couldn't afford to wait much longer. She would surely miss her bus.

Mustering her courage, Nova left her own door ajar and slunk sneakily down the hall, careful to step close to the walls, eyes trained toward the light at the top of the stairs. She made it to the banister of the stairs with little interference. Nova had a fair amount of practice with sneaking in the past; sometimes it was to break the rules, other times to avoid trouble. To an orphan, stealth is a learned life skill, and she had finally come to examination day.

Gripping the banister until her knuckles turned white, Nova gritted her teeth and took the stairs at a snail's pace. A bead of sweat trickled down her forehead. She longed to swipe it away but didn't dare risk making a sound. Reaching the bottom of the stairs seemed to take an eternity. Once on the first floor, she allowed herself a breather, but kept moving noiselessly toward the kitchen. She knew her impending expedition would be long enough she would need provisions. She hoped there was something in the cabinets that would travel well.

Upon closer inspection, she was disappointed. The cabinet was stocked with a ridiculous hoard of canned soup, the metal canisters positioned like rows of soldiers. Thrusting her arm shoulder-deep into the packed pantry, Nova snagged a bag of oyster crackers near the back and then a lone water bottle from the fridge. She didn't think a can of soup would be very practical, so she left the stockpile untouched. Remembering the wad of cash, she would probably have enough to buy food if she got hungry. Otherwise, she had gone without before.

Heading back up the stairs, Nova felt more sure-footed. The house cooperated with her, minimizing its creaks and groans as she imagined she was invisible, weightless as an astronaut floating through space. She'd made it all the way back to her door when she got cocky. Lost in her daydream about the upcoming trek, the dewy water bottle slipped from her sweaty hand, colliding with the hardwood and thudding across the floor. Nova gulped in distress and glanced toward the attic, where a shadow came into focus, growing bigger and bigger. She was found out!

Like a deer in the headlights, she watched the figure materialize at the top of the staircase. Much to her relief, it was furry and shorter than a human, equipped with alert ears and an overactive tail. Amigo listened dutifully from the attic as a strange golden shimmer reflected around his silhouette, and Nova rubbed her palms across her eyelids to clear her vision. Tingly, invisible warmth drifted down the stairs and wrapped Nova in an unnerving embrace. The hairs on the back of her neck stood on end, and she panicked as an unnatural breeze tickled her cheek. Something strange was coming from the attic. Nova's heart pounded a million miles a minute, and she took the opportunity to swipe up her water bottle from the hardwood floor and dash into her room. Her body was electrically charged, and she decided she wouldn't wait a moment longer to begin her adventure. Nova shoved the weirdness of the shimmer into the furthest recesses of her mind and sprang into action.

She hurled the water bottle into the confines of her backpack and tugged her favorite sweatshirt on in a rush, zipping it up. As her eyes scanned the room to check for any discarded belongings, she was struck by a sudden lump in her throat. Swallowing defiantly, she shrugged the backpack on and strode to the window, opening it swiftly but silently. She allowed her eyes a second to adjust to the darkness, not wanting to compromise her balance on the roof. Nova gingerly stretched a leg out the window, bracing against the frame for support. The wind was immediate, yanking on her jeans and threatening to pull her to the side. Its strength was formidable. Gripping the wood ever more tightly, Nova put her other foot out onto the roof and sat her bottom on the bumpy shingles. Fearful of drawing attention, she resorted to scooting her way to the nearest porch post, inching along like a wayward turtle. As she reached the edge of the roof, a giant flash of light illuminated the yard like the fourth of July. Lightning arched across the sky in a powerful, brilliant display.

Temporarily blinded, Nova reclined on the roof, wondering if her judgment on the escape route was sane. Before she lost her nerve, she grasped the gutter with both hands and lifted herself down to the porch post, shimmying like a clumsy monkey. The coarse grain of the wood bit at her skin, leaving splinters in her palms. She dared not drop yet. Finally, after her arms shook from the effort, she was close enough to the ground to let go. Another round of lightning sparked, and she was suddenly aware of how vulnerable she was to the view of the attic window. As soon as her feet hit the yard, she launched into a run.

As if on cue, the rain began. The gravel snapped underneath her feet as she flew up the road, raindrops stinging her eyes like tears and turning the ground into a muddy mess. Her hair flapped about her head angrily, soaked and whipping her face. Nova pulled up her sweatshirt hood and pictured the printed map in her mind. She would have to travel for a while on this road, until she hit the fork. The bus wouldn't be much farther. She envisioned the printed map, and the bus station's walkable proximity to the diner. Then, with a little luck, she would be able to buy a bus ticket and the real cross-country adventure would begin. The anticipation was almost enough to distract her from the cold rain making her clothes clingy and seeping through the bottom of her shoes. The country night was full of shadows, and the precipitation made everything look as distorted and blurred as a watercolor painting. She hoped all the monsters of the night were hidden away from the storm. Another bolt of lightning fractured the sky. The wind followed suit, racing through the trees and playing with Nova's footing. She nearly slipped as she ran, but she did not stop.

The road seemed just as long as that morning, except now she was uncomfortable in a different sense, water soaking her skin and chilling her to the bone. Nova wished she had thought to grab a blanket of some kind. With the next flash of lightning, she spied a discrepancy up ahead, praying it was the fork in the road and that soon she would be able to retreat inside the bus station, away from the storm.

In a split second of lightning illumination, something gleaming in the brush caught her eye. It glinted like a shiny green gem in the darkness. Through the howling of the storm, Nova could hear a desperate sound, soft as a whisper hidden in the grass... a gentle mewing. She stopped completely, moving instinctually to the side of the road, and reaching forward with her hands for balance. The lightning at last was useful, and when it lit again, Nova saw another flash of green—two little pinpricks of color in a washed-out world. Kneeling in the tall grass, she stretched down and plucked a tiny ball of sopping fur from the ditch. Nova held the would-be emeralds close to her face. The terrified kitten couldn't be more than a month or two old. The fragile calico body shook like a tiny leaf, and the way the little one trembled suggested it wouldn't last long in this weather. Nova unzipped her sweatshirt and placed the kitten inside, nestling it against her chest and zipping it in securely.

Nova looked wistfully toward the fork in the road. She had been so close, but she knew the kitten would not survive a trip across the country in its current condition. She would have to wait until another opportunity arose. With that, Nova turned and jogged back from where she came, her feet pounding rhythmically against the ground in time with the kitten's heartbeat. The animal's whimpers had stopped, but something inside told Nova the kitten would be all right. The emerald eyes burned brightly in her brain, acting as a lighthouse beacon carrying her back to the farmhouse.

Chapter Eight

Dakota

With thunder rolling across the fields and the rain encumbering her vision, Nova didn't dare attempt to climb back through her window. The house was as tall as Mt. Everest, and the roof was precariously slick. Her muscles shook with fatigue, and she feared falling and injuring the kitten. With a heavy sense of unease, she tiptoed across the porch to the front door, cradling the little bundle of fur in the crook of her arm underneath the folds of the sweatshirt.

Please be open, please be open, she prayed as she grasped the door handle. The handle turned easily, and she swung the door open only as far as she needed to sneak inside. She was thankful the storm was so loud; it masked any sounds that might give away her movement about the house. Her entire body felt like a wet washcloth. If someone gave her a squeeze, a river of water would rush through the hallway. With the adrenaline of her journey, Nova hadn't noticed the full extent of the saturation. The fatigue of the day hit her, and a shiver passed through her bones. Her teeth chattered as she moved like a soggy ghost up the stairs, leaving a trail of water in her wake. The attic light was still on, but the house was eerily quiet, as if it was empty of life. Consumed by weariness, Nova shouldered her way into the room she thought she would never see again. A wave of calm enveloped her.

Heading for the armoire, Nova retrieved the quilt she had seen earlier and placed it on the bed. Ever so gently, she lifted the waterlogged kitten from her sweatshirt, and began to dry it with the quilt. Though the tiny creature let out cries of distress, it didn't fight Nova during the process. As the blanket did its job, the kitten's fur became fluffy and soft. Nova was mesmerized by the kitten's beautiful markings; patches of orange, black, and white sprinkled across its little body. It looked like a smaller version of the patchwork quilt.

Once dry, the kitten stretched out her paws and pranced in glee. She rewarded Nova with a lick on the finger, and then nestled into a crevasse in the blanket. Nova felt a warm tickle play in the pit of her stomach. She had no regrets in returning to the house to care for the kitten; it had been the right choice. The little cat blended perfectly into the quilt, completely camouflaged to the eye. Glimpsing a name stitched on the quilt near the kitten's back, Nova immediately knew it was meant for the creature. "Dakota," she whispered happily to herself. The kitten purred its approval in response.

Suddenly overwhelmed by tiredness, Nova walked back to the armoire and swapped her damp clothes for a satin nightgown. The fabric was silky soft, but not at all warm. She imagined she looked like a little kid in her Sunday best with all the frills on the outfit, but at this point she didn't care. Her muscles ached as her body begged for rest. She crawled underneath both the comforter and quilt, teeth chattering uncontrollably. The last notable sensation was Dakota curling up in the crook of her shoulder.

Chapter Nine

Dreamscape

The night's sleep was a fitful one. Nova tossed and turned, teetering on the edge of consciousness. Her skin simultaneously felt as if it were on fire while taking an ice bath. The shadows in the room intermingled with her dreams and she was lost to a land of nightmares. Awareness rose and fell like a boat on the sea. Every time she came to, Nova knew she should arise to get some medicine or water, but she couldn't move. It was all she could do to ride out each new wave of sickness.

She floated into a world filled with all kinds of muted watercolor hues. Clouds of haze swirled around her, dense as fog and completely disorienting.

Violet smoke puffed past her face and ruby raindrops, alarmingly similar to blood, splattered all about the ground. Strange puddles of yellow and orange contorted nearby, melting into the surrounding landscape like acid. Navy blue flakes of ash fell from the sky and settled on her shoulders and hair. Colors shifted and snaked around her, a twisted rainbow of constantly changing shades. At the edges of her vision, the color drained away, leaving only dreadful black and white. It was as if she'd stepped into an abstract painting tinged on all sides by gray. The colors kept the gray at bay, but barely.

Within the ever-changing clouds, forms emerged; some she recognized and some she didn't. She saw the silhouette of Mr. Russell standing motionless at the top of the attic stairs, Mr. Briar's shadow as he sped away in his heap of a car, two featureless faces she had dreamt of before but had never met.

Finally, the visage of a young girl, not much older than Nova herself. This last vision brought the most pain. Even in sleep, a vast, weighted emptiness loomed within her heart, left there by her fear, disappointment... and by her greatest loss.

With this onslaught of sadness, the dreamscape changed. The gray began to drip slowly into the rest of the painting, overpowering the colors and light, erasing the forms of the people as if they had never existed. The breath was vacuum sucked from Nova's lungs as the colors disappeared. She gasped for air, but there was none. Nova dropped suddenly into a dark pit of despair, falling into a memory she'd hidden long ago.

****

Nova crossed her arms adamantly over her chest, and pressed her eyes closed as hard as she could. The blood drained from her face, and she feared she would pass out. Her world was crumbling around her, and she had to watch it happen. Emily rubbed her back in small, gentle circles, as if she were a baby. While meant to comfort her, it only fueled her anger. How dare they send her away. Tears stung her eyes and she slapped them roughly. They would never see each other again; or when they did, Emily would be grown up and not care anymore. Nova's little room closed in on her and she felt as tiny as a speck of dust. Enough was enough. She drew a deep, somber breath before opening her eyes.

Emily was watching Nova sadly. The light blonde tresses of hair crowned her face like a halo.

"No matter what, we'll always be friends. Nothing can change that."

Nova wanted to scream at her, to shake her and yell that she thought of her as more of a sister than a friend. She was losing the only person who had ever tried to understand her. The only person who she had ever loved.

Nova was at a scary precipice, leaning over the edge, about to fall. Self-defense kicked in.

"It's all your stupid parents' fault. They're horrible. I hate it here. I'll be better off without you anyways."

Emily drew back her hand in shock. Hurt was etched across her eyes. Nova felt a darkness inside her take root. She pushed off the bed and strode out the door, her face an emotionless shield. No more connections. No looking back.

****

A twinkling reminiscence of Emily's laugh echoed through the vast spaces of her mind, sinking the dagger of memory in further.

Abruptly aware once again, Nova struggled to escape this wretched nightmare. Her pulse ricocheted in her head as she fought tooth and nail to wake up, lest she disappear in this formless void... like those she'd conjured with memories. Every atom in her body was joined in a single purpose, reaching for consciousness, burning from both exhaustion and fear. Then, like a racehorse from the gate, she bolted upright and forced herself awake. She gasped frantically for air while her muscles shook. Her body was drenched head to toe in sweat. It took a moment to return to reality, but only a second for the anxiety to set in as she registered unfamiliar surroundings.

Chapter Ten

Recovery

As her wobbly vision cleared and she wiped the sweat from her brow, Nova glanced around the room. She panicked momentarily, realizing she wasn't in her Sunshine Room at all. Someone had moved her to a plaid couch in an unrecognizable place. Dark stained wood panels lined the walls of this room, the ceiling sported matching dark wood beams, and a stone fireplace sat off to the side. It crackled at her as she tried to get her bearings. Had she returned to the wrong house during the storm?

Her pulse palpated faster than the raindrops she could hear outside. A wave of dizziness crashed into her, and she was relieved to see a glass of water resting on a coffee table next to the couch. Nova gulped it down without a second thought. The cold water felt like heaven to her ravaged throat.

I must have gotten sick from the storm, she thought. Slowly, she rose from the couch, though her legs were still shaky and weak. She shuffled to the curtains on the far wall and opened them a smidge. Pewter clouds stretched across the sky, illuminated by brightness behind, suggesting that it was actually daytime. The view of the yard was nearly identical to that in the Sunshine Room, though she was level with the ground at this height. So, she was still in the farmhouse. The rain had slowed to a steady thrum, neutral white noise in the background. The storm had almost concluded. She snapped the curtains shut and ambled, reassured, back to the couch to burrow under her blanket.

Somehow, Mr. Briar had missed this room on his tour of the house. The upper half of the living room walls were painted a dark green and the space lent itself well to shadows, though it wasn't an unfriendly atmosphere. On the contrary, the firelight made the dark spots of the room dance and spin joyfully in interwoven circles. The flickering movement hypnotized Nova, and she laid back down on the couch to rest, her face bathed in the fire's glow. Never had she met a darkness so inviting. The illness softened and the heavy fog lifted from her mind while she watched the flames. They lulled her into another sleep, but now, it was peaceful and cathartic. She welcomed it wholeheartedly.

When Nova woke again, the rain had stopped. The

fire petered out in the fireplace, leaving only glowing embers and ash. Glittery sunlight peeked through the curtains. She massaged her eyes weakly and pushed herself up to a sitting position.

The living room was quiet, except for the noise of clanging dishes coming from the direction of another room. She took another sip of her water and noticed a few soup bowls littering the coffee table. They were empty, but she had no memory of how they had gotten there. Her stomach grumbled on cue, and a delicious smell wafted in from the kitchen.

"What prompted her to act so impulsively?" A woman's musical voice breathed from the kitchen. Mr. Russell was not alone. It took Nova a second to remember, but an image of recognition from the diner flashed in her mind, a bright smile and radiant golden locks. Ms. Ellie.

"She was soaked to the bone when I found her in bed. Why else would she have gone out in the storm? Her backpack was waterlogged too. I'm confident her intention was to leave." Mr. Russell's revelation seemed bruised and tender. His voice quivered like the needle of a compass searching for true North.

"You should ask her about it. Maybe there's more to the story, a reasonin' behind it." Ms. Ellie's chair scraped across the wood, and Nova imagined her standing to pat Mr. Russell on the back reassuringly. Nova felt like she'd swallowed a stone, with the weight of shame in her stomach. She hadn't meant to upset Mr. Russell.

"If she had wanted to share the details with me, she would have." Mr. Russell's voice was so low it was almost imperceptible.

"There's probably more to her than meets the eye. Sound familiar?" Ms. Ellie retorted with a low, warbly chuckle. Mr. Russell choked a laugh too. They were lost to a memory only they could see. Ms. Ellie's voice got serious. Nova leaned toward the door, straining to catch her words.

"The commitment you've made is unconditional. It's important you're honest with each other if you're going to be a family."

"I won't force her to talk to me. That's out of my hands."

Ms. Ellie clicked her tongue but stayed silent.

"The past belongs in the past." Mr. Russell's reply was sharp and final, an arrow through a target, and Ms. Ellie sighed as if she'd run a marathon.

"I'm happy to check in on her tomorrow, to be sure she's feelin' well… and you…"

"I'm fine. I appreciate it." His gruff response signaled the end of the conversation.

Nova followed the sound of footsteps mentally and waited for the tell-tale slap of the front door a few seconds later. The car in the driveway pulled out and away, engine sounds vanishing into the distance. Mr. Russell's silhouette appeared in the doorway, holding a rectangular tray laden with lunch: there was soup and even a side of crusty bread! She was shocked to see solid food in the house. He must have been really worried about her.

Mr. Russell set the tray lightly onto the coffee table and settled back facing her on the couch. He hadn't yet said a word, but his eyes spoke volumes.

They weren't angry, per say, but Nova could see they reflected his disappointment... and something else, an emotion she couldn't name. She glanced away sheepishly, hanging her head. The silence in the room was deafening.

"How long was I out?" she croaked; her whisper punctuated the awkward silence.

"A few days," Mr. Russell responded. "A rough few days. You were feverish and restless. The doctor stopped by twice to monitor your progress."

His voice grew softer. "After the second day, you started taking liquids again, which was good because you sweat out so much fluid."

"I don't remember anything," Nova said. *Except the dream*, she secretly recalled. It made her want to shiver all over.

Mr. Russell leaned forward and patted her on the shoulder. It was all Nova could do not to jump at his touch like a frightened rabbit. Human touch was a foreign experience.

Mr. Russell hadn't struck her as an involved, compassionate caregiver. His house was in disarray... a dusty, neglected mess. Yet, he'd managed to nurse an unconscious Nova out of her illness while maintaining his even temperament. He didn't even seem mad about her trying to run away, just sad and disappointed. Nova felt a wave of guilt permeating every part of her—the sensation was unfamiliar and annoying.

Due to his standoffish behavior, she assumed he didn't care. Perhaps there was more to him than she'd guessed? A door unlocked in her mind that she hadn't needed to access before; it was full of hope, gratitude, and heavy chagrin. If she was brave enough, she might be able to walk through it to a new life. She didn't know if she had it in her.

But for now, maybe one step was enough.

Mr. Russell brought her more water and opened the curtains. She forced herself to meet his eyes and eat some crow.

"I'm sorry for going out in the storm." The words tasted right spilling out of her mouth.

She smiled.

"And thank you for taking care of me."

Chapter Eleven

A Forgotten Surprise

Nova spent much of the next couple days situated on the couch recuperating. Mr. Russell was kind enough to provide her with magazines and books, though there was a limited selection intended for children. Her first pick, *Alice's Adventures in Wonderland* by Lewis Carroll, proved to be more relatable than she expected.

In the story, Alice let her impulsivity get the best of her, a circumstance Nova was only too familiar with. After reading the book in one sitting, she felt a kindred closeness to the girl who traveled down the rabbit hole, searching for something more, though she was glad to be tucked away on the couch instead of facing off against a power-hungry queen in a world filled with magical oddities. She'd had enough adventure to last her for a while.

Reading helped pass the time and when she was feeling strong enough, Nova gathered the many dishes from the coffee table and wandered into the kitchen. She placed them in the sink and realized just how involved her healing had been by the dirty soup bowl skyscrapers occupying the counter. She felt another pang of guilt and set out to find Mr. Russell.

Amigo gave him away. The dog sat still as a statue next to the garage door. Nova awarded him an obligatory pat on the head and entered, cautious so as not to disturb any of the clutter. Mr. Russell was loading painting supplies into the bed of his truck. It took him a moment to notice her standing by the door.

"Good to see that you're up." He smiled at her. "Feeling any better? The doctor left some extra medicine should you need it."

"Actually, I've improved a lot. I'm practically normal." Nova tried to sound cheery, but it seemed fake even to her own ears. She felt a knot growing in her stomach and tried to think of something to say to redeem herself and her recent poor choices. Amigo let out a whine of embarrassment for her. She shot him a glare, though he wouldn't know it.

"I'll have to head back to work tomorrow. But since you're still recovering, I thought it would be okay if you spend the next couple of days at home. I could have Ms. Ellie check on you from time to time."

Nova nodded diligently to show how agreeable she could be. It sent her into a fit of coughs.

Continuing to load the truck, he eyed her with a sideways glance.

"And speaking of Ms. Ellie, I thought we could head over to the diner tonight… to celebrate you feeling better and all."

Nova was taken aback. She couldn't believe Mr. Russell would want to treat her to anything special after she had attempted to run away. She worried it could be a trap of some kind, but she couldn't very well say no at this point.

"Sounds great!" Her voice was bubbly as a forest stream, but her heart was beating a mile a minute.

"Why don't you go change and I'll lock up the house."

"Sure thing!" And she was off, clambering up the stairs hoping not to jinx the moment of forgiveness. She heard Amigo pad behind her, resuming his job as watchful babysitter. He wasn't as subtle about it now; he could read her like an open book.

As soon as Nova cracked open the door to the Sunshine Room something seemed amiss, but she couldn't put her finger on it. Not until Amigo loped into the room did she realize what she had forgotten.

A loud screech resounded from under the bed, and a fuzzy blur zipped to Nova's feet, catapulting into the air and clawing its way up onto her shoulder. Nova fumbled to catch the kitten as she climbed, then held the creature as closely as she could, cooing at her and trying to calm Dakota's frayed nerves. Every hair on the cat's body stood on end and her attention focused intensely on the dog in the doorway. Amigo cocked his head to the side and sniffed the air, as if pondering how to respond. He let out a half-hearted bark, then turned and exited the room.

The kitten remained startled no matter how fervently Nova stroked or praised her. A new wave of guilt hit Nova in the gut as she wondered if Dakota had hidden while she was sick, with nothing substantial to eat or drink in the meantime. The kitten was practically skin and bone. Perhaps Dakota had snuck downstairs to snag some of Amigo's rations. Nova felt ashamed; a baby animal couldn't rely on wishful thinking to survive.

Nova was concocting an explanation for the new pet when Mr. Russell tapped on the doorframe. His eyes alighted on the cat and his eyebrows rose a good three inches. Nova plastered on a panicked smile.

"I... I... I couldn't leave her. It was cold and she was drenched..." Sound and sophisticated argument—not. Nova resisted the urge to hide under the bed herself.

Mr. Russell closed his eyes and drew a deep, generous breath.

"Amigo found her the morning... after the storm."

He pointed next to the armoire. Nova was surprised to see two small bowls and a tiny plastic litter box.

"I left food and water out, but she's been pretty on edge, with the new surroundings and all. I think she's going to need some TLC. She'll be your responsibility. We can pick up some extra supplies on the way home." Mr. Russell cast a dubious look Nova's way before allowing himself a tiny smile.

Nova danced around the room as he headed back downstairs. She gently placed Dakota next to the food dish, and the kitten nibbled away, content. Then Nova threw on a pair of jeans and a short sleeve shirt, grabbing her sweatshirt out of habit. She heard Mr. Russell shout up to her from the first floor.

"Be sure to close your door. Amigo's not used to furry company. Let's not test his canine instincts."

Chapter Twelve

Dinner Date

The rusty truck traipsed up the road like an old workhorse while Nova sat quietly in the passenger seat twiddling her thumbs. The night of the storm, this road had seemed sinister, foreboding, and never ending. She remembered running for what seemed like forever, her breath ragged and gasping. Tonight, a bright moon shone in the sky and the stars winked and flashed like far off lightning bugs. She rolled the window down just enough to feel the coolness of the night breeze against her cheek.

Mr. Russell watched the road dutifully, his hands resting on the steering wheel in a relaxed grip. Nova could hear the painting materials in the bed of the truck rattling around as they drove over the gravel. Behind them, the farmhouse disappeared in the darkness. The headlights shone as the only light for miles leading them on; all the scariness of the night was gone. Nova wasn't sure if it was the lack of storm or the company that made her feel more at ease. For the first time in a long time, she just allowed herself to exist at a neutral peace.

A few more miles passed, and they hit the fork in the road. Turning a sharp right, Mr. Russell pulled into the diner's parking lot; the truck creaked to a slow stop. It was the beginning of the weekend and there were numerous cars in the parking lot. The diner was busier than when Nova had first visited. The windows were illuminated from within, and the smiling faces in the restaurant resembled framed paintings. Each window told a different story. The building called forth the artist in her and Nova's fingers itched to draw the scene. She'd left her backpack at the house, so instead, she committed the image to memory by sketching the details in her mind.

It was as if the whole of the town was on exhibition in front of her. Nova couldn't peel her eyes away. There was such beauty in the simplicity of a family meal. As she stood outside the diner, staring in, she felt a piece of her deep inside dying to be a part of this tradition.

Mr. Russell opened the door and flourished a hand, inviting her in. Nova heard the happy bell and hesitated an instant, struck by the oddest feeling. It was like she was crossing a bridge from where she'd been to where she was going. All her life she had known what it was like to stand on the outside looking in. What would it be like to step inside?

She made her way with Mr. Russell up to the counter, not far from where she had originally sat with Mr. Briar. Already the car trip felt like ancient history. Mr. Russell nodded and greeted a few of the guests with a quick handshake, and then took his seat on a bar stool. Nova sat next to him and could already hear Ellie puttering about in the kitchen, sharing orders and infusing spirit into the restaurant. Ellie pushed her way out of the swinging kitchen door, and upon seeing them, broke into a delighted smile.

"Well, well, well, if it isn't my fellow pancake fan!" Her voice was lively, full of the dinner rush thrill. "Can I interest you in another helpin' of flapjacks?"

Nova couldn't help but smile back.

"I would love that," she replied quietly, still absorbing everything.

Ellie glanced at Mr. Russell, her voice growing a fraction softer.

"The usual, I presume?" She asked him.

"Of course, thank you," was his brisk reply.

She floated away, a pink flower petal bobbing on the wind. Mr. Russell rubbed his palms absentmindedly on his jeans.

"Mr. Briar called to check on you and was concerned to hear you were sick," his eyes flitted to hers. "He's called twice more to make sure you're on the mend."

"Hmmmm." Nova intoned, uninterested.

"In our conversation, I realized something important." Mr. Russell leaned forward over the countertop, reaching under the lip on the other side. He withdrew a rectangular shaped package, all done up in wrapping paper and a bow.

He cleared his throat again stiffly, continuing. "He mentioned this weekend is your birthday, and upon speaking with Ellie, I thought you might like..."

His voice petered out and he carefully placed the package in her hands. Nova felt as if she was in a slow-motion dream. Her hands moved of their own accord, and the sounds around her muted as she tactfully pulled up the tape and peeled the paper back. Within the confines of the wrapping paper was a large, glorious sketchpad. The cover was her favorite color, a deep green, as if it was destined for her. The binding was accented by gold embellishment woven across the front. Thick, textured beige pages rustled as she flipped through, almost like sandpaper between her fingers. The blankness of the book called out to her, and her fingers twitched to fill it with visual stories. A pack of graphite pencils fell out of the paper, onto her lap, their tips sharpened and ready to work. It was the kindest, most thoughtful gift she had ever received. Guilt gnawed at her heart, and she couldn't look Mr. Russell in the eyes.

"I ummm... I really... thank you." Nova stammered over her words, feeling like her mouth was stuffed full of the pancakes yet to arrive.

Mr. Russell's eyes crinkled happily as he smiled in relief. It was at that moment Ellie exited the kitchen bearing plates in her hands and on her arms, one laden with pancakes and the other a sizzling pile of fresh fried chicken. The plate of pancakes also carried lit candles, and sprinkles spelling out "Happy Birthday". Nova blew out the candles, excited, and caught up in the exhilaration of it all. She made her secret birthday wish by heart, as it was the same every year. Nova daintily set the sketchpad to the side, not wanting to dirty it with crumbs. Mr. Russell had spread out his napkin as a bib and dug into his fried chicken. Nova would have guessed soup would be his first choice.

Tucking her hair behind her ears, she removed the candles from the pancakes and mixed everything together into a scrumptious mess, pouring a healthy amount of syrup over the top. The first bite made her heart skip a beat. Sweet, sugary goodness melted into her tongue and lit up her senses. If possible, the meal tasted even better this time around. Perhaps she'd chalk it up to the circumstances. Nova didn't want to admit this was the first time a grown-up had remembered her birthday. It had never received any fanfare, and over the years the disappointment weighed on her heart. It was easier for it to stay unrecognized. The day only made her feel lonely. This was the first birthday she could recall that made her feel more full than empty. And she was grateful for that most of all.

When the plate was as blank as the pages of her new sketchbook, and the diner had grown quiet as patrons left to journey home, Nova made herself a promise. No matter what it took, her thirteenth year was going to be better than all the years before. Hugging her sketchpad to her chest and tossing Ellie a vibrant grin as Mr. Russell paid the bill, she solemnly swore to cling to her wish to belong and never let go. Like a sailor at the helm of a ship, no matter how the waves grew or threatened to toss her aside, she would hang on to this moment and allow it to guide her through... to guide her home, wherever that may be.

Chapter Thirteen

An Olive Branch

The drive home from the diner was short, but for a jaunt into the gas station to pick up some additional supplies for Nova's newfound kitten. Lost in her thoughts, it was as if the bumpy country road vanished in the blink of an eye. Suddenly they were back at the house; the tires crunched and settled on the gravel drive. As soon as the truck was in park, Nova darted out of the seat and ran into the house, clutching the sketchbook in one hand and the cat food in the other. Mr. Russell was gracious enough to carry the kitty litter. She bounded up the stairs two at a time and entered the Sunshine Room with a renewed energy. Dakota, who was resting on Nova's pillow, jumped to her feet at the intrusion. She scrambled across the room and leapt onto the armoire. Eyeing the door of the room warily, she was obviously on the lookout for her doggy enemy from before. Nova carefully set her sketchbook onto the exquisite end table next to the bed and retrieved the little blue bowl from the floor.

Nova filled the bowl with small triangular pieces of kitty kibble. She added a trickle of water from the bathroom sink to make the mixture softer and swirled it around with her finger. *Cat food soup... how appropriate for this house*, she chuckled to herself. Striding back into the room, she placed the dish next to the armoire, clicking with her tongue and speaking to Dakota in hushed tones.

"Here kitty, pretty kitty," she whispered so quietly it was barely audible, worried the cat would just ignore the peace offering. It wasn't until the kitten smelled the delicious dinner that she bravely sauntered down from the furniture and beelined to the dish. Nova shut the bedroom door as Dakota lapped up the food. She then positioned herself cross-legged on the floor next to the kitten, observing her with fascinated delight. Ever so tenderly, she placed a hand on the kitten's back and stroked her silky soft fur. The food was gone in no time, and Dakota settled back on her haunches to lick her paws clean.

It was then she realized Nova was petting her, and she turned her little head sideways to gaze up at the human. Their eyes connected for a split second, green on green. The color variation was so slight it was almost indistinguishable. Nova could have been looking in a mirror at her own reflection. In the moment of closeness, she knew she had gained back some of the kitten's trust. Relief flooded into her body like a tsunami wave.

Dakota cocked her head thoughtfully and stretched her back into a lazy curve. She padded over to Nova's legs and settled onto her lap, curling comfortably into the crease of her knee.

It wasn't until the kitten fell asleep, her breathing a rhythmic rise and fall, that Nova managed to relax. She gently picked Dakota up and transferred her to the bed, placing her onto the map quilt with utmost care. It felt good to be able to help another living thing... to make them feel safe and comfortable and loved. It was a responsibility she'd never had before, and one she took very seriously. Nova's heart was full and content, and she changed to new pajamas from the armoire with a smile on her face. Shutting off the lights, she reclined on the bed next to the quilt, her face just inches from Dakota's furry one. Her pillow was fluffy and plumped, almost as if she was laying on a cloud. Cat and child were secure together, shielded temporarily from the unpredictability of the world.

A while later, Mr. Russell cracked open the door to check on them, and the two companions were sleeping so harmoniously he thought perhaps the girl had not found the kitten by chance after all. Perhaps, the kitten had chosen the girl, and fate had known they needed one another. He patted Amigo absentmindedly and shut the door inch by inch, not wanting to disturb their well-deserved slumber.

Chapter Fourteen

The Key

Nova woke at ease, with the morning sun streaming through her curtains and a warm ball of fur nuzzled in the crook of her neck. She shifted to the side, not wanting to disturb the kitten, and stretched her arms far above her head in a satisfied way. Padding across the room, Nova opened the window to let in the day. Bird calls rang out across the fields, and the breeze smelled of grass and flowers. She took a giant gulp of air. It was intoxicating.

Dakota mewed from the pillow, her small green eyes opened bleary to the bright sunshine. Nova giggled and filled Dakota's bowl with another helping of food. The kitten didn't have the same urgency as the night before and took her time waltzing over to the bowl. While she ate, Nova trekked to the kitchen. The old house creaked in the heat of the day, the boards expanding and retracting. It sounded as if the wooden frame of the home was breathing in the morning too. It was the first time she fancied the creaking as familiar and welcome.

Nova spied Amigo curled on his dog bed in the corner as she descended the stairs. He lifted his head for a moment, and then placed it back down again, lazy and content to stay mid-nap. A plate of toast and eggs sat on the kitchen table, still steaming. Next to the plate was a note, the script long and jagged, drawn by an artist's hand.

I have some jobs today in town. Ms. Ellie will be by to check on you around lunchtime. May be a good day to give that sketchbook a try. Amigo will keep you company. Be back soon.

Nova's heart took to the sky, levitating like the wings of a hummingbird. She had the house to herself today! She couldn't remember a time when she had been in charge of her own schedule. She jumped up and down at the excitement of it all. While contemplating all the ways to spend this fantastical day, she hungrily plowed through her toast and eggs. She liked the idea of breaking in her new sketchbook. Thinking of the gift sitting so perfectly up in her room made her grateful to Mr. Russell. She decided to spend the beginning of her day doing something for him. She scrubbed her dish in the sink, and then set to work.

Mr. Russell had been kind to her in the time they'd spent together, and Nova wanted to return the favor. Feeling proud and inspired, she scoured the house searching for cleaning supplies. In a hallway closet, she located a dusty old broom, heavy with cobwebs, and a dirt-caked plastic bucket. No mop was in sight. Nova harrumphed to herself. This was going to be harder than she thought. She decided to start with the most obvious approach: beginning at the top and working down.

Grasping the old broom in both hands, she pranced around the house on tiptoe, angling it into the corners of the rooms and wrestling any loose strands of cobwebs from the ceiling. The mass of webs got larger and larger on the broom, making it look decorated for Halloween. The quarter-sized black spiders scurried hastily away, not wanting to be swept up themselves.

Once she'd hit all the corners in the house, excluding Mr. Russell's bedroom and the secretive attic space, Nova set out in search of more adequate cleaning supplies. Her hope was to clean the windows and dust the sills before she tackled the floor. She found a cloth in one of the kitchen drawers and soaked it with water. The windows were foggy with dust, and when she ran her rag over them, stubborn streaks appeared. She scrubbed at the windows for what felt like hours on end, so thick and obstructive was the film.

As she worked, the sun roasted Nova through the

glass, sweat dripping down her back and misting up her eyes. There was pleasure in the work; she enjoyed watching the grime scrape away to reveal sparkling windows and a clear view of the yard beyond. By the time she had finished the scrubbing, her arms were throbbing and sore. The windows in the kitchen remained covered with cloth, and she decided to keep them that way to spare her aching muscles.

Dakota finally ventured out of the Sunshine Room. The kitten meandered down the stairs, holding herself tall and regal, like a princess who'd just arrived at the ball. She stayed cool and collected only a moment longer, and then caught sight of a spider scuttling down the front hall. With a great predatorial pounce, she chased after the arachnid in a feverish game of tag. Amigo didn't bother to stir from his bed.

Nova guzzled down a glass of water and swiped at her brow with the back of her hand. Ceiling and windows done. Check. Now all that was left were the windowsills, banister, office bookshelves and the floor. Determination burned in the pit of her stomach, and she was suddenly struck by random inspiration. Luckily, the garage was unlocked, and she helped herself to a fresh pair of paint brushes off one of the toolboxes. Wielding a paintbrush in both hands, she set to dusting all the surfaces she could find. Nova whirled this way and that through the house, like a ninja artist, directing the dust onto the hardwood floor with a flick of her wrists. Clouds of rogue dust particles spiraled in the air, twirling in the sunlight like miniature golden fairies. Dakota meowed and leapt at the particles, adding her own frolic to the mix.

Nova threw back her head and laughed with glee.

Twisting into the downstairs office, she stopped, but only for an instant. This room was dim, but not unwelcoming. The far wall behind Mr. Russell's wooden desk was covered floor to ceiling with bookshelves. Hundreds of volumes greeted her as she entered the room, and she took great care in removing any visible webs or dust from the shelves. The paintbrushes worked well enough, but Nova found herself getting distracted from her chore by the interesting array of titles and designs. In a moment of error, her paintbrush snagged on the cover of a book, pulling it from the shelf. The book fell to the floor with a loud thud, startling Dakota, who raced out of the room. Nova set her brushes gingerly on the desk and bent low to retrieve the upended novel.

Some of the paper had creased in the fall, but the book had been well loved by the natural wear to the pages and binding. She caught a familiar whiff of wildflowers as she bent close to the novel. It was a hardcover, bound in red leather, and the gold script on the front read *Romeo and Juliet* by William Shakespeare. Nova knew a little about the love story from English lessons at various schools, but had always thought Romeo and Juliet had let themselves get in too far over their heads for love.

She reached for the book and flipped quickly through the pages to make sure none had ripped. Upon doing so, a small, metallic object dislodged and clattered onto the planks of the floor below. A key! It was an old key, made of dull brass and small enough to fit easily into Nova's palm. A thin yellow ribbon was tied to the end, a singular, modest adornment. The metalwork was simple and aged, smooth but for a set of letters etched into the handle. Nova held the key an inch from her eyes, squinting to decipher the tiny text, two capital letters… MR.

Mr.? Was it Mr. Russell's key? Why had he hidden it in the book? Nova had the sinking suspicion that the key was another mystery in a long line of secrets she was meant to know nothing about. She scrunched her nose and scratched her head thoughtfully. It had seemed like Mr. Russell considered her a part of the household with how nice he had been to her recently. But this key was a reminder he was still a stranger to her. It left her afraid of what she might find if she kept looking. It was like she was an outsider again, staring in at a world she didn't understand. Nova set her jaw and placed the key deep into her jeans pocket. Perhaps, she could figure out the secret behind it and discover a little more about Mr. Russell in the process. He had stashed it in a book after all, so he wouldn't exactly know it was missing. She would only keep it with her for a short while and see if she could find what it unlocked.

Chapter Fifteen

The Visitor

A loud series of knocks battered the silence, ringing out through the empty house like an alarm going off. Struck by a wave of paranoia at being found snooping in the office, Nova nearly dropped the book as she hastened to put it back on the shelf. She crept to the entrance of the room and examined the front door, eyes narrowed. Shutting the office door to cover up her espionage, Nova then flung the two paint brushes onto the kitchen table.

Upon opening the door, she was met with a familiar beaming smile and a cheery "Hello there!" Ms. Ellie stood on the front porch like a pretty pink rose, almost out of place against the shabby deck boards.

She appeared to be perfectly comfortable however and greeted Nova with another great big hug.

"Mr. Russell asked me to check up on you, make sure you're gettin' along fine. And I'm just tickled to see you again, Nova." Her voice was clear and true, genuine to a fault. Nova found she couldn't help smiling back.

"Would you like to come in for a minute?" she asked quietly.

Ms. Ellie looked pleased and followed Nova happily into the kitchen. She spied the cleaning supplies Nova had been using to tackle the old house. Ms. Ellie seemed impressed.

"That's awful sweet of you to tidy up like this while Mr. Russell's out." She threw Nova a wink.

Nova blushed, feeling vulnerable and, for some reason, embarrassed.

"He's been really nice to me. I thought it would be a good way to repay his kindness."

Ms. Ellie must have sensed Nova's awkwardness, because she let the subject drop, but not before giving her a tap of approval on the shoulder. Amigo appeared as if out of thin air, and Ms. Ellie laughed, amused, providing him with a pat also.

Her eyes caught suddenly on the staircase, and she let out a squeal of delight. Dakota was perched at the top of the stairs, studying the little group intently. She stood with grace, and began to make her way down the steps, curving in and out of the banister as if she were a snake. Ms. Ellie sat expectantly on the bottom step, watching the kitten with rapt attention, her face full of wonder.

"Who is this little darlin'? She is precious in every way."

Dakota purred at the compliment and allowed Ms. Ellie to stroke along her back gently. Nova was surprised at the speed with which the kitten warmed up to the visitor. She almost felt a little jealous, but only for a second.

"I found her outside in the rain. Her name's Dakota."

The kitten made its way onto Ms. Ellie's shoulder. Dakota rubbed lightly against her cheek before leaping down and prancing to the water dish.

"Lovely name for a lovely feline. She seems right at home. You must take special care of her." Dakota purred at the compliment, and Nova couldn't help but smile.

"I had a cat when I was young... Big Max." Ms. Ellie continued. "If you caught him on a good day, he'd be your best friend. Other days, he just wanted his space. Fickle creatures, cats. Hard to know what's in their hearts or on their minds." Ms. Ellie paused, then stood abruptly, eyes glassy with the memories.

"You really do have a sweetheart in her. And I can tell she's happy to call this place home."

Dakota tweaked her ears as if tuning into the conversation, batting her pretty green eyes and letting out a little meow in response. She even let Amigo give her a quick sniff on the tail before she went bounding after another spider on the floor. Nova filled with pride. The kitten really was more comfortable today. It was a notable achievement, no matter how small.

Reaching the end of the hall and bored with the

scuttling arachnids, Dakota prowled through the open front door and into the yard, arching her back and stretching long in the summer sun. Nova and Ms. Ellie followed, taking a seat in the shade of the porch on a pair of wooden deck chairs with latticed backs. Ms. Ellie reclined, watching the kitten with a mixture of glee and fascination. Nova knew this because she was watching Ms. Ellie rather closely, judging if it would be a good time to excavate some information. She decided to take a leap of faith.

"So how long have you known Mr. Russell?" Nova tossed the question into the air jovially, when in truth it was heavy as the rock in her gut.

Ms. Ellie didn't miss a beat.

"Oh, I'd reckon it was since he moved here. Going on probably fifteen years now. This place used to belong to an elderly farmer. Mr. Russell came with a new beginning in mind, and really spruced up the old place. You wouldn't know it now, but this house has come a long way. It's seen lots of years and lots of love."

Confused, Nova puzzled over her reply. Surveying the old farmhouse it was obvious that it had been many years since it had been tended. Even the yard was in shambled disarray with weeds growing as tall as the windows in some spots.

"Does his job keep him very busy?"

Ms. Ellie paused. She fiddled with a string on her skirt as she pondered the answer. At last, she clicked her tongue.

"His job... among other things. Life has seasons, and sometimes things change, even when we don't expect them to. Change can be difficult."

Ms. Ellie met Nova's eyes and affectionately grasped her hand.

"Don't judge him too much on what you see here." She gestured around fluidly. "He's been through a lot. Lost a lot too. He's a good man, and a wonderful friend."

Nova wanted to ask Ms. Ellie the extent of their friendship but found she had run out of gumption for that particular conversation. Instead, she sat silently and processed what she'd been told. Curiosity burned hotter inside her than a wildfire.

Ms. Ellie glanced down at her wristwatch and hurriedly stood up. Was it just Nova's imagination, or did she seem the slightest bit uncomfortable? What about their talk could have flustered her, with her lively attitude and easygoing mood?

"Do you need anything before I head out?"

Nova shook her head.

"Mr. Russell should be home by the end of the afternoon. I suspect he'll be pleased with all your help today." She opened her mouth as if wrestling with more words, but then shut it again.

Ms. Ellie wrapped Nova in a warm hug before descending the stairs and striding purposefully to her car; the white Volkswagen beetle was parked neatly near the end of the driveway. To Nova it looked as if Ms. Ellie were climbing into a puffy cloud.

"You take care of yourself, you hear?" she waved as she backed onto the street.

Nova waved absentmindedly back; her head was somewhere else completely. Her thoughts were racing a mile a minute with the bits of information she had obtained; she had encountered an alarming number of mysteries in this house. In her mind's eye, she returned to the office when she found the mysterious key. She was struck by inspiration as quick as lightning on a tin roof! She waited for the metallic cloud of Ellie's car to chug into the distance before she launched off the porch and raced around the house. It was a longshot, but maybe, just maybe, she knew where the key would fit!

Chapter Sixteen

How Do You Like Them Apples?

Whizzing around the exterior of the house at full speed, Nova skidded to a quick stop when she reached the large wooden gate leading to the backyard. A shiny silver padlock, about the size of her fist, sealed the gate closed. She held her breath as she touched it; the surface was surprisingly cold in the summer heat. Turning it in her hand, she could see her reflection morphed in the back of the lock, much like a funhouse mirror. She felt like a girl detective prowling after a promising hunch.

Fumbling in her jeans pocket, she pulled at the little key. It snagged on a thread in her jeans and required a good amount of effort to break free. After a moment of clumsy struggle, Nova raised the key to the padlock triumphantly, expecting a satisfying turn and click as she placed it into the lock's core. To her extreme disappointment, the key didn't even remotely fit. As she tried to turn it, it fell to the ground, nearly sliding under the fence in the process. Nova swooped down in panic! She grabbed the key to keep it from disappearing below the fence and into the backyard—out of her life forever.

Breathing a sigh of relief and holding the key firmly in her fingers, she held it up against the lock; she hoped the first attempt had been an error on her part. No, like a baby standing next to a giant, it was far too petite when compared to the lock. The metals were also of a different age. The padlock looked practically new, and the key was dull and old. Frustrated and impatient, Nova pounded the gate with her fist, sending a nearby cardinal fluttering away in absolute terror. She hung her head in defeat.

Nova reentered the house, and jogged over to the back door. The key didn't fit any of those locks either. It just didn't make any sense. With the key safe again in her pocket, she was pleased to see the dramatic improvement to the hallway and kitchen from her handiwork, though she had lost her interest in cleaning. It was blatantly obvious she'd spent significant time doing the chore. The reward bolstered her spirits and reminded her of Mr. Russell's note. He'd suggested that she try to make use of her new sketchbook. Having not drawn in the days since she'd been sick, the thought of a sharpened pencil and blank page were like a cleanser for her bruised ego. She retrieved the book and a fresh pencil from the Sunshine Room and left the house feeling inspired.

Back in the group home, Nova's art had always revolved around people. You could learn so much about an individual by watching their movements, emotions, and decisions. Some of the children had been very receptive toward her requests to draw them. They would twitch and awkwardly laugh while Nova studied their features, scribbling and erasing ferociously. It would take her time to get the proportions how she wanted them, and she made a lot of mistakes, especially in the beginning. Sometimes, her subjects would get bored, wander off, and Nova would be left with a half-finished drawing. The older kids exhibited more patience but always wanted to see the piece when it was finished. Nova had one rule about her art, especially if it had been focused on a certain person... it was for her eyes alone.

When the kids wised up and realized she wouldn't show them her pictures, their interest vanished. Out of necessity, Nova learned to adapt her art to a moving target. She had to be quicker with her outlines as she tried to capture the children playing games, sports, or going about their daily chores. She also learned to be more discrete; not everyone liked to be drawn if they hadn't given her permission. She'd found the freeform drawing had improved her focus, allowing her to take mental notes of details more speedily.

Speed was not as important out in the boonies though. Upon exiting the house, Nova stopped dead. There were no people in the vicinity of the farmhouse... or, probably for miles. She scrunched her little nose and bit her lip, instantly stumped. If she wanted to break in her sketchbook, it would have to be drawing something new. Dakota lounged on the porch, nonplussed.

Raising her hand to shield her eyes from the bright sun, Nova spied the apple trees across the road. They bore miniscule fruit, being so early in the season, but the trees were tall, mature, and still... a perfect subject for a budding artist. Nova jogged across the road, the gravel crunching under her sneakers, and settled herself cross-legged in the grass. The shade of the tree felt like a cool caress on her cheek as it counteracted the sweat dripping down her brow. Even so, the heat made her light-headed. She shed her sweatshirt and immediately felt better. Nova tucked her short brown hair behind her ears, a ritual when she would begin a new drawing, and allowed her mind to drift to the details of the tree. Her attention wandered back and forth between the bark and the leaves, much like Dakota's tail when something piqued her interest.

Nova's pencil inched across the paper, using shading to create grooves and twists in the trunk of the tree. She sketched homes for bugs and the birds that ate them, and then worked her way up the gnarled trunk in a steady, cross-hatching rhythm. The scrape of the graphite against the rough page was music to her ears and therapy for her soul.

The branches weren't as fun to draw; they were much more complicated. The shapes were all lopsided and wrong. Tongue tucked in her cheek, she erased with a passion and tried again until the lines became acceptable to her. Then, instead of drawing each individual leaf, she doodled the shape of the tree's canopy and added intricate details with curves. The leaves reminded her of veiny raindrops and were relatively easy to draw. By this time, Dakota had caught up with Nova, and was sharpening her claws by scratching at the apple tree's trunk. Nova contemplated adding her to the drawing, but her hand was starting to cramp, and the picture seemed complete enough. Holding the book out in front of her she narrowed her eyes and compared it to the tree. Mostly satisfied with the end result, Nova scrawled her name along the bottom right corner to claim the picture and gave a happy sigh. So wrapped in the satisfaction of her drawing, she didn't notice the figure approaching from behind.

Chapter Seventeen

Luck of the Irish

"*That's a pretty neat* drawin'," a voice in slow drawl mused from behind her.

Nova jumped to her feet in a flash, heart beating staccato in her chest. She slammed her book closed before spinning around.

Nova was nose to nose with a brand-new face. A boy about her age, with shocking red scraggly hair and rich brown eyes. Freckles sprinkled across his tan skin. She noticed a large gap between his front teeth when he smiled at her. The grin was friendly enough. But Nova took a step back, unnerved at how close he had gotten without her noticing. She averted her eyes and immediately began walking back across the road to the house. He didn't take the hint.

"Hey! I wasn't tryin' to scare ya. I only wanted to see what ya were up to, is all. Your name's Nova, like on the picture? That's cool." His country drawl was much faster as he became more energized, and Nova had trouble making sense of his words. She could hear him following her. He jogged into her path and planted his feet, extending his hand out straight with vigor. Put off by the boy's forward demeanor, Dakota hid behind Nova's legs.

"My name's Mac Molloy. Short for Macintosh. My pop has a sense of humor." Her face must have twisted with confusion. When Nova didn't shake his hand, he used it instead to point down the road.

"We own the farm and orchard across the way. Had the land for a couple generations. So, my name's a joke at the expense of the family business."

She blinked, befuddled. In her continued silence, he explained.

"You know... Macintosh APPLES."

She stood there blinking and feeling dumb because she couldn't think of a single thing to say. Instead, Nova hugged her sketchbook tight and studied him. His jeans were caked at the bottom with dirt. His shirt, while probably once white, had taken on a dusty brown sheen. His hair was by far his most vibrant feature. It looked like a cross between pumpkin orange and apple red. He caught her watchful gaze and gave his head a playful rub.

"Do ya like my hair?" He puffed out his chest proudly. "My family's Irish. Ya never miss me in a crowd. My Granny says red hair is where the Irish store their luck." He let out a whistle and laughed, amused by his own joke.

Feeling disquieted by this stranger's friendliness, and the fact he'd been spying on her art, Nova rushed to the porch steps and over to the door. The boy stayed where he was, wondering what he'd said to offend her. He looked like a lost puppy with his big brown eyes.

"Gotta go," she mumbled, and the screen door closed with a clang. She heard him call out as the house cloaked her in its security.

"See ya around sometime—I hope."

She answered with a slam of the door. It was harsher than she intended; but at least it sent a message. She did not have any room in her heart for friends. Her past had taught her not to rely on them.

****

A four-year old Nova laid like Superman in the dirt, on her stomach with short legs stretched behind her, fingers caked muddy as she traced imaginative pictures into the soil. This backyard was small, with a chain-link fence and patches of abused grass throughout. The traffic blared and screeched on the nearby busy street, but for Nova, the world was silent. She wiggled her fingers in the dirt like worms, but intentional, with an image in mind. Her nails were brown and dusty; when she itched her forehead, a muddy streak was left behind like a birthmark. She tried to make three round circles, but the dirt was difficult, and her snowman looked more like snow puddles. Nova grabbed a prickly stick from the ground and dug into the dirt, scraping indentations deeper and deeper with impassioned determination.

So entranced, she didn't hear the door to the house slam shut and the malice-filled voices of children sneak up behind her. Something struck her in the back of the head, the same weight and size of a well-placed spitball. Nova rolled onto her back in time to see another missile launched through the air. To her disgust, a giant roly-poly bug landed on her cheek, its jerky legs finding purchase on her skin and clinging for dear life. She shrieked in fright and immediately rolled horizontally, flat as a log, across the ground, shaking and squirming to dislodge the insect. The two rotten brothers hooted and hollered at her reaction, then searched the yard for more bugs to throw. Nova bounced furious to her feet, hair disheveled and wild, her face cherry red from the embarrassment. She bit her lip and tried not to burst into tears.

"That's not nice," little Nova insisted, wagging a finger at the boys and stomping her feet.

"You're the weirdo playing in the dirt with the bugs. We're just having a little fun." The older of the two scowled at her and crept closer. He had a millipede wriggling in his pudgy fingers, and Nova jumped into defense mode. Raising her hands in front of her face, Nova lashed out with her foot and caught the boy square on his knee. He yowled in pain and screamed for his mom, his younger brother frozen like a mime, with his next buggy grenade held aloft. Nova's toes stung from the kick, and she winced as she walked on them, but she raised her fists defiantly at the brother, who then backed slowly away, dropping the bug and retreating into the house. Nova turned and limped back to her snowman, but the scuffle destroyed all evidence of the drawing. All that was left was blank, untouched earth.

The first home she could remember; the first time she was sent away. The first of many disappointments in a long history of being alone.

Chapter Eighteen

Unfortunate Habits

After her run in with Mac, Nova felt jittery. He had caught her off-guard and brought up some painful memories; ones she would have preferred to be left buried deep. Now, she paced the floor flustered and nervous, peeking every few minutes out the window to see if anyone remained outside the house.

Her paranoia was so tangible that eventually she moved into the living room where there were thick curtains hung across the glass so no one could see in. Eager for a distraction, she turned on a lamp and settled herself onto the couch. She had selected a book from the end table titled *The Secret Garden*. The vines woven across the cover struck her as similar to the design of leaves upon her little table in the Sunshine Room.

She opened the book with shaky fingers and allowed herself to be transported away, through the ink, to a world very different from her own. So lost was she in the pages she didn't stir when Amigo and Dakota clambered up onto the sofa; they stretched into the crevasses of the couch for a comfortable snooze. Nova must have made it halfway through the book before she was startled back to reality by the sound of a key in the front door. The doorknob rattled as it opened, and the fog of reading lifted from her brain. She replaced the book on the end table and skipped to the kitchen, anxious to show her cleaning handiwork to Mr. Russell.

He stood in the front hall stooped over like he was scrutinizing his shoes. His hand was braced against the wall as if the house was holding him upright. Mr. Russell had the demeanor of a man twice his age in the way his back was bent, like an invisible weight rested on his shoulders. Nova took a step back.

When he finally staggered into the kitchen, his gait was slow and shuffled. He tossed his coat onto the chair and dropped his keys on the table, not even giving Nova a sideways glance. The smell coming off of him was one she recognized and cared not to dwell on; it was sour and rank on his breath. Some of her previous caretakers had sported that smell on a regular basis, and she knew from prior experience to steer clear of an adult who had filled their belly to the brim with liquor.

Mr. Russell ambled over to the fridge and grasped at the handle. It took him a couple of tries to find it, but when he did, he pulled it open and grabbed a bottle from the back of the top shelf. It was then Nova found her voice.

"I could put on some soup or something. I haven't had dinner yet either." Her suggestion was quiet, but hopeful enough she prayed it would shake Mr. Russell from his predicament.

He laid wide eyes on her when she spoke, as if realizing suddenly she was present. There was an empty glaze in his vision, and it seemed as if he could hear her, but his brain took extra-long to process her words.

"Not all that hungry. Thanks anyway." His voice sagged as he attempted the stairs. Nova's eyes moistened with a hint of tears as he made his way up to the attic without a word about the state of the house, or a question as to how her day had been.

Her sadness quickly turned to anger, and she bolted up the stairs to her room, whipping the door closed behind her. Looking for something to kick, her foot connected with the leg of the bed—not once, but twice. She succeeded only in adding a new bruise to her toe.

There had been a part of her that had been optimistic about the house, against all of her better judgment. She had thought it was far enough removed from the world that the problems of mankind may not be able to follow. But inevitably, the shoe always dropped. She had learned a valuable lesson over time. The only person she could trust was herself. The

Sunshine Room and the drawing book had broken down her walls, but in her current disappointment, she felt the achy emptiness of solitude return. She'd hatched a plan her first night in the house, to get back where she really belonged, and perhaps it was time to revisit said plan. She wouldn't be as impatient this time around. She would have to wait for the right moment, the best opportunity to be successful. Nova had officially made up her mind. It was only a matter of time until she took charge of her own life.

This house was not destined to be her forever home.

Chapter Nineteen

Up Above

Nova was restless well into the night. She considered drawing another picture, but her hands were too anxious and jumpy. She couldn't keep them still. She rearranged the hangers in her armoire and organized the contents of her backpack, tucking each item into a new pocket for the sake of keeping her mind occupied. Her anger bubbled just below the surface, and she did her best to keep it from spilling over. The effort made her feel twitchy all over, like she was covered in chicken pox. Nova scratched at her arms and legs, trying to sooth the itch.

Then she flung herself onto the bed, arms splayed above her head as she studied the lines in the ceiling.

She didn't think she would ever get over the betrayal she felt from Mr. Russell. A piece of her had hoped he would be different, that this would last. It didn't matter, though, as eventually she would move on, and these moments would fade into her past like a ghost into the mist. She turned on her side and begged for sleep. Sleep was uncooperative.

After an hour of tossing and turning, Nova braved a jaunt into the hallway. Mr. Russell's bedroom door lay open and his bed empty. The light to the attic blazed down the stairs like a spotlight, the only brightness to be found in the midnight shrouds of the house. Nova could hear clattering from up the stairs and the garbled mutterings of someone both drunk and distracted. Mr. Russell sounded agitated at the world. Retreating back to her room, she shut the door soundlessly and set her resolve.

It took another couple of hours of fighting her droopy eyelids for Mr. Russell to finally descend the stairs. She could hear his heavy footfalls even with her door closed. He didn't wander down the hall to her room. Instead, she discerned the sound of another door closing. Risking a peek, she confirmed he had shut himself into his bedroom. Amigo was nowhere in sight.

As driven as Nova was to do some sleuthing, she willed herself to wait some more, until Mr. Russell had actually fallen asleep. It was well into the early morning hours when she dared to make her move. Nova had always been a quick learner, and she was becoming familiar with this house. She knew that three steps into the hallway there was a squeaky board and she avoided it with ease. She took care to keep her feet from scraping across the coarse wooden floor and held her breath as she reached the bottom of the attic stairs. The hairs on her neck stood on end as she ascended the staircase, journeying up above into the unknown. The third-story room was pitch black. Nova had difficulty finding her footing with the last few steps. She felt a tickle on her cheek and panicked, holding back a scream, only to discover that it was a pull string to a light bulb as she grasped it in her palm. Feeling sheepish, she gave it a tug. Light flooded into the space and, involuntarily, she gasped.

The room was maybe twenty feet long, with a decorative stained-glass window situated at the end. The attic was devoid of any clutter or mess, contrary to the rest of the house. All the walls were an unpainted oak wood gleaming in the light of the fluorescent bulb. The wood smelled reminiscent of warm honey and made her feel instantly at home. Lofty ceiling rafters were peaked and airy, making the room seem like the inside of a church. Nova could faintly hear the crickets chirping outside as their sound reverberated off the tall ceilings in a muffled chorus. The acoustics of the room were impressive. The floors were swept and polished, and only three pieces of furniture occupied the area; a storage chest propped against the side wall, a custom wooden easel in the center of the space, and a stool placed in front of it.

It's a studio, Nova realized as she took a tentative step forward. As soon as her foot hit the landing, a force engulfed her, like she had stepped into an invisible, pulsating cloud of energy. There was a palpable electricity in the air, vibrating around her, resonating through her from the top of her head to the tips of her toes. The entire room hummed gently, the thrum of it massaged her entire body, instantly relaxing her. Butterflies circled in her stomach, and she swallowed great gulps of air. It was as if the room was alive. She felt this place wasn't meant for her, like it was a secret hideaway, and the exclusivity caused her a momentary pause. The warm energy swept from the floor to the ceiling and back again, like a playful wind, always moving, exploring, and changing. She had never felt such a thrill in her life, and she could not reasonably define the magic of the studio. Bathed in a golden glow from the bulb in the ceiling, and perhaps something more, Nova knew for certain this attic was sacred. Yet, she'd come too far to turn away.

Chapter Twenty

The Easel

Positioned directly in the middle of the room, the handcrafted wooden easel was a pristine shrine. She tiptoed toward it so as not to make any of the floorboards creak. Her worries were unfounded; the floor was secure and solid under her feet. When she was next to the easel, she could feel the heat spilling off of it, like stepping into a dense tropical fog. It instantly made her relax.

The wood was smooth and stainless, and appeared practically new. The vertical slats stood tall and straight, with intricate carvings running up and down their length. Every piece of wood was connected by golden brackets and screws. The tray for the canvas sat primed and ready for future art, scrolls of woodwork adorning its sides. There was not a drop of paint anywhere on the structure, which surprised her considering how long Mr. Russell had spent up in the attic, presumably working on something. Nova longed to reach out and touch the easel; it was so beautiful. Her uncertain hand hovered for a moment, but then she dropped it. Something held her back. Maybe later.

Growing bolder, she made her way over to the storage chest by the wall. Nova pulled at the brass handle of each drawer and alcove, revealing a vast array of paints, brushes, towels, scrapers, and blank canvases. The cabinet was meticulously arranged. Every compartment was lined with red velvet cushioning, and each tool sat poised and proud in a designated spot. Nova hadn't known Mr. Russell was capable of such organization. Or perhaps the art supplies simply remained untouched, and he spent his time upstairs on other matters. She wasn't sure.

Nova felt the familiar pull of desire toward the brushes and paint, her fingers dancing to a familiar tune only she could hear. She desperately wanted to create something with these supplies, and the easel drew her like a magnet. It beckoned her closer, speaking to her in a language that only an artist could understand. It took all of her self-control to close the drawers and walk away.

Looking back from the stairs, the pull string in hand, Nova felt anticipation rise inside of her... something was waking up. She couldn't abandon this house without figuring out what made the easel so special, or she'd spend her entire life wishing she had investigated it more. She would bide her time until she was truly alone. The risk was too great with Mr. Russell still in the house. If he discovered her in his sanctuary, she would surely be banned from this place. She knew it in her gut. This was his biggest secret, and one he had not wished to share. It wouldn't be long before his job took him away again, and then Nova would find out what made this room tick. Patience had paid off before, and she was confident in its value. Even so, turning off the light and hauling herself down the stairs felt like ripping off a bandage, so sharp it almost stung. She knew she could never go back to her mindset before she'd found the attic.

Her head replayed the events of the day as she was hit by a wave of exhaustion. Traipsing back to the Sunshine Room felt like a mile long hike, her eyelids drooping and ready for sleep. She didn't notice Amigo nestled in the shadows; silent and watchful, his milky eyes trained on her path. He cocked his head thoughtfully and sniffed the stairs to the attic before settling down outside of Mr. Russell's door. Nova was asleep as fast as her head hit the pillow. But Amigo was wide awake and alert. Dogs have an intuition after all; it's a wild instinct that can usually sense when a metaphorical storm is coming. Beyond his animal instinct, Amigo's loyalty knew no bounds. He had a stringent duty to his master. He rested his big, fluffy head on his equally fluffy paws, and released an audible sigh. It would be a long watch.

Chapter Twenty-One

Plan B

Nova woke from her short-lived sleep like a patient coming out of a coma. She had to drag her eyelids open and force her body out of bed. Her late-night escapade in the attic had deprived her of rest, but she didn't want Mr. Russell to know. So, instead of sleeping in as her fatigued body demanded, she readied herself at the break of dawn to greet the day.

After changing into a pair of jeans and a t-shirt, Nova stifled a yawn and fumbled down the stairs to the kitchen. She nearly stepped on top of Amigo, who had sprawled out across the landing, his giant furry body acting as a barrier between the attic and Mr. Russell's room. The bedroom door at the end of the hall was ajar, but only slightly. Mr. Russell hadn't surfaced yet, so she took a few minutes to splash some water from the kitchen sink across her face. She clapped her hands on her cheeks in rapid succession to jolt herself awake. Dakota perched like a gargoyle on the windowsill. The kitten glanced at Nova sideways through slitted eyes with a look of incredulity—as if questioning her sanity. Nova ignored her and smoothed down her bedhead just as Mr. Russell entered the kitchen, Amigo hot on his heels. She plastered on a smile as she foraged through the cabinets, not wanting to look too eager for conversation.

Mr. Russell didn't know what to do with himself. He paced to the front door and back, clearing his throat and making a show of checking his watch. At long last, he let out a big sigh and settled at the kitchen table with an empty mug waiting for the ancient coffee pot to summon him. When he finally did speak, he sounded embarrassed.

"I was in quite a state last night," he whispered, playing with a broken thumbnail. He couldn't meet her eyes. "I just want you to know that I don't plan to make a routine of it, is all. I don't know what more to say than that."

Nova had been around the block enough to know when a grown-up had a habit like Mr. Russell's, it wasn't something he could turn on and off. A laugh of disbelief rose up in her throat, but she squashed it down. Still, she dug through the pantry, keeping her back turned to the table. She nabbed an old granola bar from the depths of the cabinet, and tore it open, nibbling like a mouse and leaning on the countertop.

"I used my sketchbook yesterday," she smoothly changed the subject, neither forgiving him nor feeling ready to address last night. The change of topic caught him off-guard.

"Oh... good..." Mr. Russell's voice faded away as the coffee pot gurgled to life. He was just as uncomfortable, because he moved swiftly to the counter and poured himself only three sips of coffee. He limped back across the kitchen pathetically, like a wounded animal.

As he rinsed out his mug in the sink, he spoke once more.

"I've got to go into town to finish the job from yesterday. If you want, we could do something fun when I get back. Maybe go fishing on the pond?"

Nova forced an agreeable grin on her face, though bile rose in her throat. The idea of touching a slimy fish was not her idea of fun, but she didn't want Mr. Russell to doubt her interest.

"Sounds like a plan," she tossed her wrapper in the trash without throwing so much as a glance his way. Then, she sprung up the steps two at a time, careening into the Sunshine Room. Poised by the window, she watched slyly as Mr. Russell backed his truck out of the garage and puffed away down the dusty road. Nova didn't release the breath she had been holding until he was out of sight. She threw her arms above her head and twirled across the floor like a ballerina, enamored with the feeling of being on her own and then succumbing to the dizziness. She giggled as she toppled onto the bed. Dakota mewed at her from the doorway, cocking her head to the side, concerned by the girl's antics. Nova's enthusiasm was immeasurable. She gave Dakota a tiny rub on the head as she exited the room.

Now that Nova was alone, she could finally get to the bottom of what was going on in the attic! She wanted to comb the space from top to bottom. Something in her gut told her Mr. Russell was a man of many mysteries, and Nova had learned to put faith in her instincts.

Unfortunately, once in the hallway, she screeched to a halt.

Amigo had parked himself once again at the bottom of the attic stairs. His unseeing eyes glinted with determination and were trained directly at Nova as if they were looking into her soul. It sent a chill up her spine. She scrunched her nose in thought and whistled softly.

"Amigo, come. Who's a good boy?" Nova made her voice light and playful, like she wanted to start a game of fetch. It sounded forced.

The dog's ears perked up, but otherwise, he was a statue. His large body seemed as big as a brick wall, and Nova knew she wouldn't be able to sneak past him. She would have to come up with a different plan.

It came to her quickly enough. Lacing her shoes up with purpose, she made a show of grabbing her art supplies before heading back into the hallway. Making as much obvious noise as possible, she descended the stairs with Dakota tailing her close behind.

"The weather is PERFECT today." Nova intoned, a little more loudly than necessary. "Don't you think we should take advantage and practice some sketching?"

Dakota played along, prancing after Nova and batting her tail to and fro. Out of the corner of her eye, Nova saw Amigo get to his feet. She beelined for the front door, praying he would follow suit.

Positioning herself comfortably onto one of the deck chairs, she opened the sketchbook and doodled absentmindedly. She had only finished the outline of the gravel road when Amigo pushed his way through the screen door and hunkered down for a nap in the sunshine at the base of the porch stairs. Nova allowed herself a self-satisfied grin but kept drawing. Gradually, Amigo's breathing slowed. She watched his chest rise and fall peacefully, and she knew it was time to make her move. Channeling her inner cat, she balanced on the balls of her feet and sprung across the porch as nimbly as she could, launching into the house and slamming the front door behind her. The latch of the lock on the door was music to her ears. Now, she could get to the bottom of the secret attic.

When Amigo realized he had been tricked, he scratched ferociously at the front door, whining all the while. When his efforts were not rewarded, he started to howl. He sounded so distraught Nova almost felt bad for leaving him outside.

Almost.

She justified her actions by rationalizing it was Mr. Russell's fault for keeping secrets. If he had been honest and upfront with her, she wouldn't have to go to these lengths to know the truth. Amigo was the collateral damage.

Skipping into the Sunshine Room, Nova stashed

her sketchbook under the bed with her other possessions. As she withdrew her hand, a piece of paper floated out from the inky shadows. Nova recognized it instantly and was struck with a bittersweet nostalgia. Ever so gently, she lifted the paper and folded it carefully to place in her pocket. Her hands were shaking, but she knew with certainty she was going to use the easel. Inspiration was a fickle thing, and for an artist, it could strike at any time. Steely with resolve and ignoring Amigo's continued howls, Nova excitedly ascended into the attic, knowing precisely what she was meant to paint.

Chapter Twenty-Two

Shimmer

Nova's progress stalled when she hit the top of the stairs. The aura of the room was so powerful that it took her breath away. Once again, she discerned the attic was faintly glowing from every floorboard, rafter, and wall with a warm incandescent light. The air pulsed with the light as a frisky wind circulated through the attic, tugging at her clothes to say hello. Though Amigo could still be heard howling outside, the sounds were muffled and less startling. Nova felt her muscles relax, and she allowed herself a pause. She let the warmth of the space fill her up, closing her eyes and reveling in the inexplicable calm. From her very core she could feel the attic was a safe space. It made her never want to leave.

When she again opened her eyes, there were tears at the edge of her vision waiting to spill out. She wiped them away and withdrew the piece of paper from her pocket. It was her most prized possession, and she braced herself for the pain of examining it. Fingers trembling, she unfolded the picture and was met with a striking array of bold, beautiful colors, melded together to form the image of a detailed butterfly. It was like no real butterfly she had ever seen, stitched together by a rainbow of shades. There were more colors to it than she could count. The drawing was concocted with colored pencil, yet somehow, the different colors married together as paint would.

There were many times Nova had looked at the butterfly to remind herself that she was not alone. It was the most valuable gift she had ever received. The paper was crimped and folded from being manipulated over time, the edges curling up slightly as it aged. She traced the initials at the bottom of the paper with her forefinger, slowly and methodically, having done so dozens of times before. *EB*. She trembled with an onslaught of regret, sadness, and loss. As much as she loved the butterfly, she had to look away.

Progressing over to the cabinet, Nova selected a few different thick and thin paint brushes, and a plastic palette to hold her paint. The velvet lining of the drawers tickled her fingers as she sought out the supplies. She was careful when squeezing the paint out of its tubes, as she didn't want to take so much Mr. Russell would notice it was missing. Her heart raced in her chest, the beats pounding in her ears. She slid onto the stool in front of the easel and placed a square canvas into its arms.

Nova started to doubt her plan and her ability the moment she picked up the paintbrush. She had practiced with pencils before, but all of this felt so foreign and new. Not only that, but she was an intruder in Mr. Russell's personal sanctuary. She hadn't asked permission and risked losing his trust. Worst case scenario, he would send her back to the home and never want to see her again. Her chest felt heavy, weighted with the possibility.

One thought kept her going forward: she had come this far.

If she was living in this house, she deserved to know the whole story. She locked her fears and inhibitions deep away in her mind, as she'd practiced over the years. Nova then selected the first color for the butterfly, a vibrant yellow akin to the Sunshine Room. With her special drawing clipped to the top of the easel, Nova paced herself recreating the image. She lost herself in the movement of the brush strokes; swaying back and forth, she conjured the butterfly's curves and edges. Her lines were not as meticulous as the picture, but there was a beauty to them all the same. She wiped the brush on a towel to clean it when she needed to switch colors and added dots of shadowing where necessary. Occasionally, she would scamper to the staircase to view her painting from afar. The whole experience was beyond refreshing. Nova felt more at peace than she had in a long time. This peace was particularly surprising because she had never been able to look at the drawing without overwhelming sadness. The minutes turned to hours, and gradually the canvas transformed into a representation of a butterfly. Nova stepped back for a final time to assess her work. Though it was not an exact copy of her precious picture, she was proud of the level of detail she was able to achieve.

The eraser was an essential part of her regular drawing process. Any mistakes could be easily remedied or adapted. Painting was a different experience entirely. To fix mistakes while painting, she had to consider the best ways to cover them up. She made some errors in the painting that could not be undone, but she combined the misplaced colors in such a way they became an integrated part of the art. She subconsciously knew they were there and wished she could make them disappear.

Overall, for her first painting ever, she was surprisingly pleased by the finished product. She used the smallest brush to etch her first name into the bottom corner of the canvas. Nova then held it up with pride to study it some more. She couldn't stop smiling, a lovely crescent from ear to ear.

Nova jolted out of her reverie when Amigo started barking again from the front porch. It didn't sound as urgent as his howls earlier. She snuck to the window and craned her neck to see out.

Mr. Russell's truck was making its way up the road, back to the house. A stone dropped into the pit of her stomach. He was early. This was the worst-case scenario. She would lose his trust.

Bolting from the window, Nova nabbed her drawing, the palette, the dirty towel, and the paintbrushes.

In her haste, she did not have time to hide the painting. She would have to keep Mr. Russell out of the attic until she had the chance to retrieve it. Skidding down the stairs, she launched into the bathroom and tossed the brushes into the sink. Water on full blast, she scrubbed them as quickly as she could. Glancing over her shoulder every now and again, Nova strained to hear Mr. Russell's entrance over the slush of the faucet. Amigo was continuing to bark, and now, faintly, she deduced the bang of a car door. Not enough time!

Wrapping the paintbrushes in the dirty towel, and covering the palette the same way, she leapt into the Sunshine Room and stuffed the supplies under her bed, then sprinted toward the stairs. She heard the front door open and Amigo's paws scuttling on the hardwood as he finally gained entrance. Her cover story was already taking shape in her mind.

Nova's eyes were wide and alarmed, her hair looked wild atop her head from her frantic race. She patted it down and tried to compose herself before bounding down the stairs to the kitchen.

Show time!

Had she been paying more attention, she may have noticed that Dakota remained on the top step to the attic—entranced by light dancing about in the room. The kitten's eyes glowed gold with the reflection from the easel. A hazy shimmer of effervescence descended from the tip top of the easel across the painting. The golden glitter looked like a cloud of fireflies blinking in a nighttime field. The entire canvas lit up momentarily; so brilliant was the shine, Dakota had to turn her head to look away. When she looked back, Nova's artistry was gone. The canvas sat, clean and crisp and untouched, atop the easel. The butterfly had vanished into thin air.

Chapter Twenty-Three

Taking the Bait

Nova was oblivious to the miracle Dakota had witnessed in the attic. She was distracted as Mr. Russell trudged through the front door, jingling his car keys, and hanging up his work jacket. She had to act natural, or he would discover she had been snooping.

Amigo sat in the kitchen, glaring and huffing in Nova's direction. He stuck his nose in the air and let out a breathy, ear-splitting whine. She did her best to ignore him.

Mr. Russell started the conversation.

"Is everything all right?" he looked quizzically between Nova and Amigo, sensing the tension.

"Right as rain!" Nova could have slapped her palm to her forehead at the expression. Natural indeed.

"If Amigo is going to spend more time outside, we'll have to put some water out with him. It's a scorcher here in the summer."

Underneath his request was a question, and Nova had to slow herself down so as not to rush the answer.

"Oh, yes. I should have thought of that. He and Dakota weren't getting along earlier, so I had to separate them for a bit. I should have remembered to give him something to drink."

She crossed her fingers behind her back and hoped he would take the bait.

Mr. Russell scratched his chin and considered her reply. Eyebrows raised; he gave Amigo a pet on his head.

"It's Amigo's first time sharing the house with another critter. He's got to learn how to be more welcoming."

Amigo whined again, clearly put out, and in disbelief his master could be so gullible. Nova thanked her lucky stars that he could only speak dog.

"Just be sure that he isn't alone too long. He enjoys companionship too."

Nova nodded enthusiastically, so quickly she tweaked her neck. Rubbing the back of her neck, she stuck her tongue out at Amigo when Mr. Russell turned to leave the room. To his credit, Amigo had fantastic intuition. He let out a small growl at Nova's display of disrespect.

She knelt down and whispered gently into his ear, instantly regretting her cruelty and realizing he would be better as an ally.

"I'm sorry, okay? I just know something is going on here, and I have to figure out the truth."

Amigo laid his head on her shoulder, but she could feel he was still tense. It would take her ages to earn his loyalty again. That's the price she had paid to gain access to the attic.

Mr. Russell re-entered the house just as Nova got to her feet. He held two fishing poles out in front of him and had a tackle box balanced under his arm.

"What do you say we take advantage of the day and try to catch some fish?"

Nova's stomach trapezed across her ribcage, but she knew she needed to keep Mr. Russell away from the third floor. She gave him a half-hearted thumbs up and a smile while she checked the lacing on her shoes.

Mr. Russell wasn't kidding about the reeling summer heat. Upon exiting the house, Nova was hit in the face with a blast of boiling air. Droplets of sweat gathered instantaneously on her forehead, and she wiped them away with her hand. Shielding her eyes from the bright sun, Nova surveyed the yard and the old gravel road. The gravel shone white in the light of the day, like someone had taken a paintbrush of purest ivory and run it across the green fields. There wasn't a car or another person to be seen for miles. Nova turned and squinted as she peered the opposite direction; that's where the boy, Mac, had said his family lived, in the middle of the orchard. She could see the tops of trees in the distance, but that was all. In an effort to relieve the growing heat, Nova pinched her shirt with her fingers and wiggled it, allowing the air to flow through. She would have to be more careful with the animals. Amigo must have cooked out here.

She heard Mr. Russell maneuvering in the garage. Though he proceeded with caution, the mountains of cans and junk swayed precariously as he moved past. He held up a small styrofoam cup.

"Found some worms, just in case."

Nova tried not to gag and opted for carrying the fishing poles. She followed him around the side of the yard and along the perimeter of the fence. She ran her hand along the fence as she walked, careful not to get a splinter, but enjoying the rough texture of the wood. Amigo trotted behind them at a steady pace, panting, and happy to be included.

"The pond'll help with the heat. There's always a nice breeze out there." Mr. Russell was visibly excited about fishing. His voice was the most energized Nova had heard yet. She couldn't pinpoint why. In her thirteen years on this Earth, she had never once cared about going fishing. She still needed time to abduct the painting in the attic. So, at least this was a useful way to stall.

As they got closer to the pond, the grass grew taller and wispier. Nova spotted some cattails and water lilies along the banks of the pond. She jumped a full foot in the air when a frog that had been sunning on a rock decided to swan dive into the water. Dragonflies glided across the pond, swiveling like little helicopters. She could hear the familiar hum of insects going about their microscopic business. There were even some ducks paddling in the middle of the water. Every so often, they would dive down in a secret chase. Resurfacing again with a bill full of algae and tadpoles, they quacked happily at their aquatic feast.

Nova itched to draw the pond. It was so natural and pure she almost didn't mind the marshy smell or the bugs buzzing about her sweaty forehead. Mr. Russell approached the water's edge, parting the long grasses to reveal a small wooden boat resting on the shore. Amigo clambered in and reluctantly, Nova boarded also. She gripped the edges of the boat until her fingers were sore. She had never learned to swim, so she prayed there were no holes in the hull, or that the pond wasn't too deep. Mr. Russell gave the boat a small shove and hopped in himself, picking up the paddle and steering it with confidence. The ducks took to the air as the party drifted closer. Amigo barked at their sudden flight.

Despite herself, Nova found the pond air was genuinely refreshing. She took great gulps of it to fill her heat-stifled lungs. Then, she dipped her hand down into the cool water, wriggling her fingers through the pond and mimicking the motion of the ripples. She could see fish darting about in the water, their silver scales flashing briefly before disappearing into its cobalt depths. Mr. Russell demonstrated how to put the lure on the end of the fishing line. He tied the knot quickly and with the ease of many years of practice. Nova was relieved he hadn't opened the container of worms.

The boat spun gradually with the current from the breeze, almost as if it was taking part in a slow dance. Mr. Russell took her fishing pole and swung it back over his head before flinging the lure into the water a good distance from the hull. He showed her how to grip the rod in a way that was both comfortable and secure. Nova's brain was a sponge absorbing everything he told her. She was so engaged in the lesson that all the events of the day were long forgotten.

It took no time at all for the tell-tale tug on her pole. Nova catapulted to her feet in excitement, nearly toppling out of the boat. Mr. Russell laughed and coached her through the painstaking process of reeling in the fish without breaking the line. She could see the fish splashing out of the water as it pulled with all its might. Nova patiently guided it toward the boat, her exhilaration building with every inch.

When at last she could haul it up and over the side, she was beaming with pride! She had never seen a fish so close before, at least outside of a tank. Its small, beady eyes were round as bubbles and silky black. The gills opened and shut as it searched for water to breathe. She had thought the fish would feel slimy, but instead it was smooth as a polished pebble. She took a snapshot with her mind, willing herself to remember all the details so she could draw it later. Mr. Russell clapped her on the shoulder as she released it back into the pond. The fish dashed immediately away.

The next couple of hours were full of laughter. Mr. Russell moved the boat across the pond when they had exhausted a specific fishing area. Amigo would perk his ears every so often at the wildlife surrounding them. He spent most of his time snoozing in the shade under the seats. Nova settled into a rhythm with the fishing; reel, catch, release. She didn't even mind when Mr. Russell switched out her lure for an actual worm. She looked away as he strung it on the hook, but was happy to see the fish so eager about the fresh meal.

She appreciated that they could share each other's presence in silence. Nova discovered Mr. Russell was also capable of having fun. He knew more fishing jokes than she could count, and her giggles repeatedly woke Amigo from his slumber in the bottom of the boat. Nova became so comfortable she inadvertently let her mind wander to memories long forgotten.

"I've never been fishing before today," she spouted breathlessly as she picked a duck feather up off the surface of the pond. She stroked at its tendrils, admiring how soft they were.

Mr. Russell cracked an eye open. "Is that so? Any particular reason?"

"Well, I visited the aquarium once, but I never had the opportunity to go fishing. The aquarium was different. All of the fish had bright colors, like pastel paints. And they lived in beds of coral. We even saw a shark while we were there!"

"It sounds like the experience stuck with you."

"My foster family made it a point to take me along, for a while. They believed education to be, and I quote, 'the most important thing.'"

"They're not wrong," Mr. Russell smiled amicably.

Nova would have smiled back, but she was disoriented by the memories.

"Not long after, they stopped taking me with

them. I had a friend in their daughter, but eventually I was sent back to the home." Her voice had fallen to a whisper, and she pulled at the little feather in her palm, ripping off tiny pieces and dropping them to the wind.

Mr. Russell studied her thoughtfully. "That had to have been difficult."

Nova turned away from him to face the house. "It's been my normal," she intoned, but the light had gone from her eyes.

There was a long pause now, and it seemed as if Mr. Russell wanted to say more. Nova didn't dare turn back to look at him. She didn't want to see the pity in his gaze.

"Well... I think we've exhausted the fish for one day. I don't know about you, but I'm starting to get hungry! How about we head back to the house and make some dinner?"

Nova gave a little nod and discreetly rubbed at her eyes with the back of her hand; she felt angry for reasons she didn't understand. Nova didn't trust herself to speak without her voice breaking. Mr. Russell took up the paddle again, strong and steady, and steered them back to the shore. As they stepped onto the grass, Nova glanced wistfully at the pond, wishing the good times could last forever. She'd been through too much to believe they could. The pond remained picturesque, even in the impending darkness. She was grateful for its quiet, timeless beauty. Maybe it was enough holding onto the memory.

Chapter Twenty-Four

Keyhole

Upon arrival at the house, Nova ducked up the stairs while Mr. Russell braved the garage to put the fishing equipment away. Her deception flooded back to her as they had approached the house, and she was frantic to retrieve the painting from the attic. She chastised herself for forgetting it in the first place. More of a shadow than a dog, Amigo was hot in pursuit as she bolted up the stairs. When she pulled the drawstring for the light, her stomach dropped. The painting was gone, and a blank canvas rested on the easel. Nova was taken aback.

Mr. Russell had to have visited the attic before going fishing. Had he seen the painting and relocated it? He already knew she had betrayed his privacy and trust. Nova dug her nails into her palm and bit her lip, immediately distressed. She searched her recollection of the day, trying to determine if he had seemed upset on the fishing trip. There was not a single instance she could pinpoint where he had let on that he was disappointed. She had actually thought he was enjoying himself. Either he was a very talented actor, or he didn't care she had snuck into his attic retreat. She couldn't decide which was less believable.

Clicking out the light, Nova took the stairs two at a time and took refuge in the Sunshine Room. Pacing like a caged beast, she tried to think of a plan. She wasn't prepared to leave again in the middle of the night, but she couldn't risk being sent back to the home either. If she went back, she would have lost her opportunity to escape. So now she had to figure out the best way to handle Mr. Russell.

At that moment, he shouted up the stairs.

"Are you good with peanut butter and jelly for dinner? It's one of my favorites from when I was a kid!"

"Sure, sounds good!" Nova quickly hollered back, analyzing his voice for negative emotion. Frustratingly, he was cool as a cucumber.

Fearing she would give herself away, Nova locked herself in the bathroom to settle down. Her reflection in the mirror put all of her internal stress on display. There were dark shadows under her eyes, frown lines on her forehead, and her mouth was set in a scowl. She poked at her face aggravatedly as she schemed.

She would need as much time as possible to think of a viable excuse for sneaking into the attic, so for the time being, she would pretend it hadn't happened. She wouldn't say a word until he brought it up. Her brain moved at light speed as she ran through the scenarios in her head, every possible conversation with a corresponding response. Nova felt like she would overheat at any second by the speed of her conjectures. She forced herself to take some deep breaths.

Mr. Russell had set the table when she made it down to the kitchen and was already digging into his PB&J. Nova tried to flop casually on her chair and chew normally, but she kept side-eyeing her caregiver, trying to gauge his mood. He seemed happy enough, licking the jelly off his fingers. Nova was wound up tighter than a coiled spring.

The state of high alert lasted until she holed up in her room at the end of the evening. Even then, she remained stir crazy circling the room and waiting nervously for Mr. Russell to throw open the door, tower over her and accuse her of betrayal. Dakota looked nonplussed reclining on one of Nova's bed pillows, washing herself methodically with her tiny pink tongue.

Nova craved the calm she had found in the attic. Though she had never painted before, it had been an unforgettable experience. She wished she could do it again, but she wasn't daring enough to try. Better to lie low for a while to make sure her position in the household hadn't been compromised, so she'd be ready when the time came to leave.

Pushing off the bed, she wandered over to where her sketchbook lay on the decorative end table. She considered trying to draw something, but her hands shook nervously. Her gaze lit on the pretty table that held the sketchbook. She had loved it the moment she'd seen it. Now after having tried to paint, Nova had a new appreciation for the artistry of the design. The vines and flowers seemed professionally detailed. Nova couldn't believe the intricacy of the images, from the hair thin outlines to the shadowing done on each of the petals. Whoever had painted this table knew what they were doing. She traced her hand along the image, following the curve of the vines over the tabletop and down the side. Her palm came to rest on the side of the table, and she felt a strange ridge she hadn't noticed before. Leaning down, she peered cross-eyed at a tiny metal keyhole set into a small drawer, previously hidden from view. Nova fell backward onto her bottom with a thud and gaped in surprise. It was as if a ghost had jumped out and said "BOO".

Launching toward the bed, she burrowed through her secret treasures underneath, unearthing the key she had found in the library. Her treachery forgotten in this moment of triumph, Nova held her breath as she inserted the key into the side of the end table. Her anticipation rocketed the moment she heard the little click and turned the key to the side. Ever so carefully, she inched the drawer out of its hidey-hole. A cloud of dust loosed from the interior, as if it had been shut for many years. Nestled in the confines of the wooden drawer was a stack of envelopes yellowed with age. She lifted them from their hiding place and brushed off the remaining dust; she caught a whiff of memory as she did... the paper smelled of fresh cut wildflowers.

Nova tried with all her might to remind herself she was pushing her luck. She had already snuck into Mr. Russell's attic. Would opening these envelopes be the straw to break the camel's back?

A little mischievous voice inside her head took charge, tamping down her good sense and pushing her onward. He hadn't ever opened this drawer. There was too much dust and age to it. He probably didn't know the letters existed. They may even have been inside when he bought the furniture. She ignored the fact the key had been stashed in his library. Besides, if she put the notes back inside the drawer and locked it again, what harm could looking at them do?

Hurriedly, she wrestled on her pajamas and settled into bed. Laying and watching the letters all the while, she was worried they would disappear like her painting in the attic. Nova snuggled into the mattress and tugged the comforter up to her chin. When she could wait no longer, she selected the top envelope and opened it with care. It was not sealed or ripped. Had it ever been sent anywhere? The front of the envelope was blank but for the number 1. Fingertips trembling, she tugged the letter out of the envelope and began to read.

3 de Septiembre de 1991

Van Gogh,

I am so glad you sent that letter. Explaining it to Mama was a chore, but I am grateful to have the chance to talk to you across the miles. It seems like years since we met in the park, though it's only been a week. When you were here, it felt like freedom was in my grasp. Now, my house is a makeshift prison, courtesy of my parents. I hung your painting of me above my bed, as a reminder that creativity means possibility. Please keep writing.

Sincerely,
Mari

Chapter Twenty-Five

Insanity

Nova woke herself with a loud snore and a start. She had fallen asleep sometime in the night, with the letter she was reading propped up against her face like a sleep mask. The dust from the paper tickled her nose and she let out a sneeze.

Pressing her hands to her eyes and releasing a giant yawn, she scooted out of the bed and started gathering up the letters. Luckily, Mr. Russell hadn't come in to wake her this morning. The envelopes were strewn about her bed haphazardly, like a mail tornado had spun through the room.

She placed the letters back in the drawer and smoothed them down before pushing it closed and turning the key. Nova pondered stashing the key under the bed with her other belongings, but it seemed far too obvious, and her guilt had her feeling paranoid. She would have to be cleverer. Opening the doors to the armoire, she stepped up onto the cabinet shelf, stretching her arm as high as she could. Nova wobbled precariously on her toes and thrust the key behind the molding at the top of the armoire. Leaping down, she closed the armoire doors again with haste and let out a deep sigh, hands resting lightly on her hips.

A tiny mew echoed out from behind the curtains in the bay window. Nova turned and smiled. She could see Dakota's shape through the sheer curtains, outlined by the bright morning sun. The little cat's tail flicked back and forth, and she crouched down on all fours, as if she was stalking prey. Nova yanked back the curtains, prepared to squish the spider Dakota was hunting.

Only there was no spider. Nova yelped in surprise and stumbled backward. Dakota, momentarily distracted, cocked her head in Nova's direction and meowed again. Nova clutched at her heart with her hand and her mouth gaped open. The sight that waited for her was unexpected, to say the least. She had to pinch herself to make sure she was awake.

Drifting upon the breeze outside her window was the most illustrious, dazzling butterfly she had ever seen. Three times the size of a normal insect, it looked as large as a bird. Its wings glittered in the rays from the sun and boasted a rainbow of colors and patterns. Opening and closing its wings hypnotically, the butterfly alighted lazily on the roof of the porch. Nova pressed her face against the window, astonished. Her breath fogged up the glass and she scrubbed it clean again with her sleeve. The movement startled the butterfly, and it took off into the air.

Scrabbling to the bed, Nova dug under the duvet for her coveted drawing. Sure enough, when she unfolded the paper, the butterfly pictured was identical to the one she had seen outside. Gripping the paper firmly, Nova thrust open the bedroom door and skidded down the hall. She careened out the front door in three seconds flat, blue pajamas and all. She spun like a dancer on the gravel driveway, blocking her eyes from the sun and looking frantically for the mythical vision of a butterfly she had to have imagined. The garage door was open, and Mr. Russell's truck was gone; he must have left for a job that morning. She stepped back into the road to get a better vantage point. It just so happened, Mac was strolling up the road at the very same time.

Nova could only imagine how she looked, gawking in the middle of the street in her PJ's with bedhead running rampant through her hair. She blushed ever so slightly as Mac approached, but remained fixated, continuing to search for the butterfly.

As he drew closer, Mac raised his eyebrows toward the sun.

"Is everythin' alright?" he asked cautiously, as if he didn't really want to know the answer.

"I... It's just..." Nova stuttered like she had gum stuck to her tongue.

"THERE!" She shouted, wildly pointing her finger in the direction of the backyard. The butterfly sat poised on a fence post, ruffling its wings, clear as day.

She grabbed Mac by the shoulders and spun him around toward the fence. He yelped in surprise.

"Do you see it? The butterfly on the fence?" Nova squeezed his shoulders a little too tightly, and he swatted her hands away, annoyed.

"Um, yes." He seemed unimpressed.

"So it is real. I can't believe it!" She mumbled to herself in a low voice, running her fingers through her hair and tossing her arms above her head in amazement.

Mac studied her with a wary gaze.

"Are ya sure you're feelin' well?

Her chest rose and fell in deep gasps. Nova felt her breath catch and fought to keep from fainting. She wondered briefly, *Is this what a panic attack feels like?*

"I... don't know." She lowered herself onto the spiky grass on the side of the road, training her eyes on the butterfly, attempting to find a rational explanation.

Mac looked like he wanted to sit next to her, maybe pat her on the shoulder. But, instead, he wandered closer to the butterfly trying to see what all the fuss was about. When he got too close, the insect rose into the air, and hovered over the fence for an instant before vanishing into the backyard.

Mac retreated back to where Nova had plopped down and positioned himself in the grass a few feet away.

"It's a weird looking bug, I'll give ya that. Why's it got ya so spooked?" Nova could feel the heat of his gaze on her face. She blushed again. She must have lost her mind. Finally, she met his eyes. Her own were filled with doubt and anxiety.

"You wouldn't believe me if I told you," she whispered.

In response, Mac stood, rubbed his palms on his jeans and scratched thoughtfully at his head. Nova assumed he would turn away, walk back down the road and leave her alone in her insanity. That's what she would have done if she kept company with a crazy person. Surprisingly, she had no desire to see him leave in her current state. At this moment, she needed a friend to hold her steady.

Instead of abandoning her, he reached his hand down to her, his fiery hair burning red like a ray of the summer sun. A charming, cheeky grin played about his lips as he motioned her to her feet.

"Try me," was his singular and decisive reply.

14 de Septiembre de 1991

Van Gogh,

Not much has changed since my last letter. I had an argument with my father yesterday. Sometimes, I think he wishes he never had a daughter. I'm expected to fall in line to fulfill my family's whims. But what about mine? I know that they want what's best for me, but how can I follow my dreams without following my heart?

I've made good progress in the book I was reading that day we met. Do you recommend any others? Romeo and Juliet's story may have been a tragedy, but at least they were true to themselves. Your letters are helping me to move forward despite all this chaos. Always keep writing.

Sincerely,
Mari

Chapter Twenty-Six

Boys

Clasping her hand firmly in his, Mac led her into the house. He pulled out a chair for her at the kitchen table and brought her a glass of water to sip. Nova spotted another note from Mr. Russell on the table, detailing he would be out on a painting job until mid-afternoon. It provided her a smidge of relief knowing, for now, she wouldn't have to pretend in front of him. She hadn't figured out what she was going to say to Mac about the butterfly. Instead of speaking, she buried her face in her hands.

Mac's presence in the house put Amigo at ease. He splayed out in the front hallway, not at all concerned by their comings and goings. Dakota, on the other hand, was hyper alert. She sniffed Mac's sneaker curiously under the table while staying hidden, so she didn't actually have to make social contact. Mac was busy examining the decor, or lack thereof, in the house. His eyes breezed around the kitchen, patiently waiting for Nova to share her confession.

"It's this house..." she began in a whisper, playing with the condensation on her glass and keeping her eyes trained downward.

Mac didn't speak, so she continued.

"It's always felt a little... off to me. And when he gave me the tour, he didn't take me up to the attic."

"Grown-ups like their secrets." Mac stated matter-of-factly.

Nova nodded, hesitating to reveal the rest of her story. Eventually, the words just spilled out of her like an avalanche.

"So I went in the attic to check it out and it's a studio."

"Makes sense, Mr. Russell bein' a painter and all."

"I thought so too, but he mostly paints buildings. I like art, and I got bored, so I went up to paint yesterday." She left out the part about not asking permission.

"Anddddd...?" Mac leaned forward in anticipation.

"And... I painted a butterfly."

He rested his chin on his hands, measuring her up skeptically.

"Seems kind of anticlimactic, don't ya think?"

Nova got exasperated, her voice increased in volume and became pitchy.

"No, you don't get it. I painted THAT butterfly. The butterfly outside. I left the canvas on the easel when

Mr. Russell got home because I had to get out of there. When I woke up this morning, the butterfly was waiting for me outside my window. Almost like... like..."

"Magic?" Mac finished her sentence breathlessly. His eyes were as big and round as golf balls. Now he sat stock still, absolutely frozen. The impact was setting in, she could just tell.

Before she could blink, he burst out laughing.

"Ya had me going for a second. Phew. You've got a real poker face, ya know? You're going to have to teach me how to do that sometime."

It was as if someone had struck a match and lit her on fire. The blood rushed to her face, and Nova stood, impassioned, shoving the chair back in frustration with more force than she meant. A shocked Dakota dashed up the stairs like a fuzzy bullet fired from a gun.

"FIRST YOU TELL ME YOU'LL BELIEVE ME, AND NOW YOU HAVE THE NERVE TO THINK I'M LYING?"

Her voice reached a new octave, but she didn't care. She was so angry she could spit.

"What do I have to gain by lying about this? It makes me look like a crazy person!"

To his credit, Mac only slightly cowered, his face an ashen shade of gray as she laid fury into him. He looked remorseful enough, but he wasn't a pushover.

"Hey now. No need to shout. Ya said yourself it's hard to believe. I thought ya were havin' some fun."

Nova crossed her arms and glared at him, the poster child of icy stares.

"Okay, okay," he raised his hands in a gesture of peace. "It could very well have been a coincidence the butterflies looked the same."

"You said yourself it was weird." Nova insisted.

Mac paused at that.

"Hmmmm... I did."

Struck by inspiration, he bounced to his feet.

"Let's try it again!" His cheery disposition reignited in a flash.

"Again?" *Oh, no.*

"Yeah, to test if it was a coincidence. We can paint somethin' and see what happens. It's the scientific thing to do." Mac pumped his arm in the air, convinced it was a foolproof plan. Nova incredulously tried to disagree but couldn't think of a good reason to fight with him.

"What if Mr. Russell finds out?" She asked half-heartedly.

"Pssshhhh, he won't be home for hours." Mac gestured to the note and gave her a wink. "I can read too."

Were they really going to do this? Ironically enough, Nova's stomach filled with butterflies at the suggestion. Painting the first picture had been risky, but any picture completed now would be downright irresponsible. She didn't know the how or the why of the easel, but her gut told her it wasn't a toy. Mac had laced his fingers together like he was going to beg her if she told him no. She supposed she could always blame him for the idea.

Plus, it would be reassuring to know she wasn't out of her mind.

"Oh, fine." She gave in with a disapproving frown and an almost imperceptible twitch of her head toward the staircase.

"But don't say I didn't warn you!" she called after him as he skipped up to the third floor without a care in the world. Nova followed him, mute, up the stairs; her feet had turned to lead. Each step felt like a marathon. This was the payoff for honesty. Somehow, she'd been cornered and tricked into a very stupid decision. What had she gotten herself into?

Rolling her eyes, one word rebounded through her brain.

Boys!

Chapter Twenty-Seven

Mistakes Were Made

It was clear Mac had way more enthusiasm for their top-secret project than she did. He was a pinball in the attic, pinging back and forth between the easel and the cabinet, talking energetically about the task at hand. Nova tried to squelch her sinking feeling of dread. It was so intense she couldn't manage to participate in the brainstorm with him.

"...we should make somethin' that's actually magic, to prove if the easel really works..." Mac rifled through the drawers of the cabinets as if he were browsing a library, taking his time perusing the compartments and studying all the materials.

"My Granny used to tell me stories of the old

country—Ireland. Fairy tales mostly. I wanted to hear scary stories, but she usually kept them pretty mild." Dakota appeared like a spirit at the top of the stairs, followed by Amigo. Amigo fixed Nova with a furtive stare, as if to say 'I'm here to stay'. He then laid his massive body on the hardwood floor, resting his head with a huff upon his furry paws.

"She always claimed when she was a young girl, she had seen a real leprechaun outside her family's cottage."

Nova immediately tuned into the conversation.

"A leprechaun? Like, the green man from Lucky Charms?"

Mac belted out a brief laugh.

"Ya would think so, but no. She always described leprechauns as tricksters who wore red, not green. Though they collected gold and stuff, hid it at the end of rainbows, they were really greedy and kind of malicious."

Nova scrunched up her nose. "Malicious as in evil?"

"I mean, they're tiny people. How evil could they be?" Mac was alarmingly undeterred. "Besides, Granny loved to embellish." He fished tubes of paint out of one of the drawers, amassing a sizable pile of options on top of the cabinet. Clearly, he would need some boundaries.

Nova inserted herself between Mac and the cabinet.

"If we're going to do this, we're going to be smart about it. That means..." She placed some of the paint back where it had come from. "We limit the amount of supplies we use."

"Have it your way then." He wandered over to the easel where the blank canvas still rested from the other day. It gave Nova the heebie-jeebies to think about how the painting had been there and vanished without a trace. Was it really possible for art to come alive?

"Just be sure ya get red and gold paint. Granny was always very insistent about leprechauns not being green. Then again, there were days she thought she was still in Ireland, so who's to say she really knew which way was up."

Nova squeezed minute amounts of paint onto another plastic palette. She selected a thick and a thin brush to use, and then remembered the dirty items hidden under her bed. Handing Mac the palette and brushes, as well as a cloth for switching colors, she left him to start the picture. He seemed eager to give it a whirl.

Nova took the opportunity to dig up the painting supplies she had used yesterday, and give them a good scrubbing in the bathroom until the palette and brushes were spotless. Once she had changed into jeans and a t-shirt, feeling exceptionally embarrassed to have been caught in her PJ's, she carried the supplies back to the attic studio. Mac was making ample progress on the outline of his picture. The proportions were a little wonky, but you could definitely see the shape of a small man. It looked like Mac intended to give him a long red coat, complete with golden buttons and two deep pockets. He stuck his tongue out of his mouth as he splashed new colors onto the canvas while concentrating fiercely on the painting. Nova suppressed a giggle.

She came up beside him and admired the continuity of his strokes. Pointing at the canvas, she also gave him a few helpful hints, showing him where to add shadows or highlights. The whole process was tedious, but effective. After about an hour, the picture was nearly complete, and the children were exchanging wisecracks back and forth.

"Please, you can't tell me that this isn't a self-portrait." Nova placed her hands on her hips in jest.

"It's a leprechaun! I'm not a leprechaun!" Mac was just as stubborn.

"The hair is the exact same color as yours. It even has your freckles."

Mac tapped the brush to his chin thoughtfully, dabbing some paint there by accident.

"Of course!" He exclaimed. Wielding the tiny brush, he added a small goatee to the leprechaun's chin. The patch of hair did its job. Now it didn't resemble Mac... but a Mac twice his actual age—and miniature.

Nova let him have the victory.

Mac reclined on the stool with a smug expression.

"I'd say for my first paintin', it's pretty good." He made a rectangle with his hands to take an imaginary snapshot of the painting.

Nova gave him a playful shove on the shoulder. She was surprised at how much she was enjoying his company.

"Don't go getting a big head!" She teased him. "It does look like a leprechaun, so it fits the bill."

"What now?" Mac asked.

Nova let out a shrug and gathered the supplies to wash up again. Best not to leave any tracks.

"How am I supposed to know? I haven't ever actually seen anything happen."

She left Mac in the attic; he hopped in front of the painting like the white rabbit from that Alice book. Nova had gotten halfway through her cleaning routine when a holler rang out from above.

"Nova! Get up here! NOW!" Mac's voice had an unnatural sense of urgency.

Dropping all the supplies in the sink, Nova sprinted up the stairs.

The entire studio was bathed in a golden light, and a glittery shimmer descended upon the canvas. Mac had backed away from the easel, his mouth gaping open. The shimmer began to sparkle so brightly that both children had to cover their eyes and look away. The air felt warm and comfortable like a summer breeze against Nova's cheek. She even thought she could smell the spray of saltwater, like this attic wind had kissed the ocean. When she could again focus on the canvas, Mac's leprechaun had vanished. A stunned silence filled the room.

"This is... impossible..." Mac spoke in a shaky whisper. He looked like Nova had felt earlier, as if he was ready to faint. Or throw up. Or both.

"Let's see what happens. Follow me!" Nova hustled down the stairs, out the front door, and around the side of the house. She couldn't see above or below the fence. Mentally cursing all the locks and latches, she found herself wishing she could open the back door at will. Now she had an explanation for why Mr. Russell locked everything.

Mac followed her as if he were sleepwalking through a dream, at a distance in slo-mo. Nova couldn't blame him. It had taken her a while to accept this reality too.

They made it to the back of the fence as a dense, mysterious fog settled over the top of the pond. The fog lazily drifted toward the backyard, easily skirting over the fence and vanishing beyond. The wind momentarily picked up and blew leaves off the treetops. Nova examined the fence intensely, wishing she had x-ray vision and looking for any type of gap to catch a glimpse of what was going on. The craftsmanship was quality, and she had no luck. Mac stood, dazed and silent, next to the fence. You could see the battle going on in his head written across his features. He pulled at his ear in an anxious tic. To be honest, he looked frightened.

"You haven't lost your mind." Nova told him reassuringly. "We're probably going to have to find a way to climb this fence."

A series of deep barks and growls rang out closer to the front of the house. Amigo was in a frenzy and Nova knew it was no coincidence. The noise woke Mac from his stupor.

"That's gotta be it!" he proclaimed.

Side by side they raced toward the house, pumping their arms for speed and rounding the corner to find absolute chaos had ensued.

It was at that moment Nova realized they had made a grave mistake!

Chapter Twenty-Eight

Hooligan

Nova and Mac skidded to an abrupt halt and immediately realized they were in over their heads. The scene in front of them was like something out of a movie. As they had rounded the bend, a tiny man hurtled over the fence gate and landed bowlegged in the front yard. His dark eyes glinted mischievously in the powerful afternoon sunlight, and he stroked his goatee while surveying the landscape surrounding him. He was dressed in a fancy scarlet overcoat with gold thread and sparkly buttons. His feet were clad in black leather boots, which he tapped on the dirt like he was dancing an Irish jig.

Amigo's barks turned to angry snarls. Though he couldn't see the leprechaun, his sense of smell was keen, and he knew an intruder was in their midst. The leprechaun paid no attention to Nova and Mac, and they remained paralyzed in shock. He skipped in Amigo's direction, amused by the dog's outbursts. Then, light as a helium balloon, he swept through the air and onto Amigo's back, resembling a cowboy on a bucking bronco. Amigo spun and kicked, snapping his jaws at the leprechaun's feet, but the tiny man threw up his hand and whooped with glee.

"Hooligan." Mac muttered under his breath.

The word broke Nova from her trance. "Huh?"

"It means troublemaker." Mac blushed briefly. "It was Granny's nickname for me."

"Well, I've already had enough of this hooligan. Come on. We have to do something. Amigo may never forgive us if we don't."

Nova careened up the porch steps and into the house, shouting back to Mac.

"Quick, let's hide the gold!"

She prayed he caught on, and that the leprechaun was listening in too.

Rummaging as quickly as she could through the kitchen drawers, Nova nabbed the first golden object she could find, an ancient, dusty wrapped piece of candy that was probably older than Mac's Granny.

Squinting one of her eyes shut to aim, she thrust back her arm and released, bringing the candy forward and tossing it like a teeny bowling ball. It rolled across the kitchen, through the front hallway, and into Mr. Russell's office. Nova hoped the shine from the wrapper was enough to entice the leprechaun to investigate.

Sure enough, as she hid behind the railing of the staircase, she saw the little man appear as a silhouette in the front door. Amigo was nowhere to be seen. Fingers crossed he had run for cover as soon as the leprechaun had dismounted. Now, the hooligan was tiptoeing across the entryway toward the office door, snickering to himself in an otherworldly voice. Nova held her breath.

The leprechaun entered the office unaware of the deceit, but when Nova stepped forward toward the door, a floorboard squeaked. The little man whirled around and shook a finger at her, as if to say 'you can't trick a trickster'. He dove for the hallway and Nova's heart stopped. She was too far away.

At the last second, Mac appeared out of nowhere and brought back his foot like an olympic soccer player. Mac's sneaker caught the leprechaun in the stomach, hoisting him into the air and sending him flying backward into the office. Mac gave the leprechaun a formal salute, before pulling the door closed and bracing himself against it, both hands on the knob. Nova could just make out the leprechaun's anger at being trapped before the door closed; smoke could have billowed from his ears with the intensity of the scowl on his face. Thank goodness Mac helped in time.

Still, the leprechaun hadn't surrendered. Mac's whole body trembled as the door shook and shimmied, his hands visibly slipping with sweat while the doorknob rattled ominously. Nova yelped and rushed to his aid by grabbing the brass handset over his grip and adding her weight. After a minute or two of testing the door, the leprechaun grew bored and quieted. The children were too hyped to relax. Their hands stayed glued to the door, just in case.

"Well, this has been a fun day," Nova remarked flippantly.

Mac craned his head as he scanned down the driveway, keeping his fingers around the knob out of caution.

"It's not over..." his voice trailed away as Nova heard the familiar crunch of tires out front.

Oh no!

Mr. Russell was home.

"Can you stay by the office? I want to break it to him slowly." A lump of fear rose in her throat.

Mac nodded and gave her a sympathetic glance.

Nova dragged her feet to the front of the house, feeling exhausted. She tried telling herself Mr. Russell would forgive her, but she didn't believe the pep talk. It wasn't until she forced herself onto the porch that it occurred to her that Mr. Russell wasn't her main concern at the moment.

Mr. Briar stepped out of his outdated black car, briefcase in hand, giving her a little wave as he fumbled with the seat belt.

Nova heard the crash from inside the house and fought the instinct to turn around. Reluctantly, she plastered a smile on her face. The shenanigans weren't over yet.

5 de Octubre de 1991

Dear Van Gogh,

I'm sorry so much time has passed between our letters. I was working on a special project. I could only whittle at night, when the rest of my family was asleep. I found a craft book from the library that showed me how, but it still took me a few tries. You would have laughed to see the monstrous results of my first couple of paintbrushes.

I borrowed the hair from one of our horses, and molding it to the right shape was a challenge. The carving was much easier for me. If you check, you'll see marigolds, morning glories, and sunflowers along the handle, just like we saw together in the park. I was hoping to give you a piece of Mexico, and to inspire you to keep painting. I know that sometimes your studies discourage you. You have a true gift for art, and it would be a crime to waste it. Please keep writing to me as well. It makes the days seem exciting and new.

Sincerely,
Mari

Chapter Twenty-Nine

Home Review

Mr. Briar crunched up the driveway as he glanced warily around, presumably on the lookout for Amigo since their first meeting had been less than amicable. He had not yet noticed the cacophony of noise ringing out from the house. Thank goodness the walls dampened the sound. Nova met him halfway up the drive, stopping him in his tracks.

"Hi, Mr. Briar! What a great surprise! I didn't know you were stopping by for a visit." She had the habit of getting sing-song when she was nervous. She hoped he couldn't tell.

"It's good to see you too, Nova. It's customary to complete a home review after the first couple weeks of placement." His voice was formal and scripted, as if he'd repeated these statements a zillion times before. "Usually, we'll pop by unannounced so we can get the full scope of how our charges are adjusting to their new residences."

He raised his eyebrow at her, breaking from the script. "This isn't your first home, Nova. Certainly, you're used to the protocol?"

Nova cleared her throat and stood her ground, shifting from foot to foot to block his path.

"Oh, of course, Mr. Briar. Don't be silly. It's all routine to me! I was just hoping you could come by when Mr. Russell was home. He was called out on a job, so he won't be home for who knows how long."

Mr. Briar's eyebrows rose another inch and he started scribbling on his notepad.

"Is that so?" He muttered under his breath, taking his sweet time writing. Nova's pulse quickened and her hands got all twitchy. Perhaps this wasn't the best tactic.

"He works soooo hard to provide for me, Mr. Briar. He's always committing to jobs and taking on extra responsibility. Besides, I have a friend over today, so I haven't been lonely at all."

Nova's voice died out at the end of her rant, and she could have slapped her forehead in self-disgust. The caretakers were very strict about supervised socialization, and Mr. Briar spent enough time coordinating with them that he shared many of the same rules. Nova may as well grab a shovel from the garage and start digging a hole to hide in, with how smoothly she was handling the exchange. Instead, she just itched the back of her head and grimaced. Mr. Briar continued to write.

"Be that as it may, we're required to complete a certain number of visits prior to the conclusion of the first month to ensure the well-being of our charges." Back on script again. "Perhaps you'd like to take me for another tour? Fill me in on how everything has been going?" He clicked his pen with finality.

Nova tried to mask the dread creeping through her bones.

"Oh, of course! But it may be terribly boring! The house is much the same as when you dropped me off, though we have been cleaning a bit!"

Mr. Briar examined her suspiciously. Cleaning was not a normal part of her agenda. He knew that. She knew he knew that. She wished she had a sock available to stuff into her mouth to make this less awkward. Her main concern presently was keeping Mr. Briar from entering the office in hopes the leprechaun would not be sprung.

She attempted to lead him toward the backyard. He cleared his throat.

"Let's start inside, if you don't mind. The air in my car still hasn't been fixed, and it's a hot one today."

Nova strained a laugh, though he hadn't told a joke.

"Duh! Naturally, we should go inside first."

She led the way up the porch stairs, her brain spinning, her muscles tense and achy from anxiety. As she crossed the threshold to the house, Mac was reclining casually against the office door, as if he didn't have a care in the world. He was bouncing a ball on the floor; Nova wondered briefly where he had found the toy. She determined Mac was a better actor than she was.

He confirmed that theory. Raising his hand in greeting, he gave Mr. Briar a million dollar smile.

"How's it goin'? Name's Mac. Nice to meetcha!" His tone was so upbeat Nova wondered if he'd suffered a bout of amnesia.

Mr. Briar paused for a moment, scrutinizing the boy. He looked like he wanted to object, but to his credit, he spared Nova the embarrassment.

Instead, he shook Mac's hand, the boy pumping his arm up and down with vigor. Mr. Briar promptly let go, flexing and shaking out his fingers, appearing slightly put out.

"So good that Nova's made some friends. Always a sign of healthy adjustment. How long have you two known each other?"

Mac's chirpiness was contagious, and Nova felt herself relaxing against her better judgment. An ominous thud from the office quickly snuffed out the pending comfortable feeling. Somehow, Mac didn't react.

"Well, sir." Smooth. "I met her when she was drawin' outside one day. She's got talent with a pencil. She's probably the best kid artist I've ever seen."

Mr. Briar nodded, vindicated by the response. "You're right about that, my boy. She has a natural ability."

It was the kindest compliment he'd ever given her. If only she wasn't about to have a panic attack and hyperventilate. The thumps in the office grew more frequent and louder, as if the movement happening in the room got frenzied. It didn't take Mr. Briar long to notice.

"Is there a problem? I thought you said Mr. Russell isn't home."

Nova opened her mouth to speak but no words came out, only an eloquent squeak. She would owe Mac big time.

"He's not, sir. I was keepin' Nova company today. In fact, I'm helpin' her train her new kitten. Little creature's full of energy. We shut her in the office so she can calm down."

Mr. Briar leaned closer to the door to listen. The thuds had stopped, but out of nowhere there was a clamorous crash. Something fragile had most certainly met a painful end.

"Should we check on the animal?" Mr. Briar asked reluctantly, not a fan of pets. Nova was pretty sure his twitchy eyes continued glancing around for Amigo too.

"Better to let her relax there for a while." Mac insisted, and he drove the dagger home. "She doesn't always get along with new people." He drew his finger across his throat in a scratching motion. Mr. Briar gulped, looking practically disquieted and pale as a sheet.

"I have to go to the bathroom." Nova suddenly announced, sounding skittish. "Mr. Briar, I don't want to hold you up. You can tour down here while I'm gone."

She met Mac's eyes and wordlessly pleaded with him not to abandon the door. The corners of his mouth twitched in understanding, like he found the whole thing funny, and she had to hold herself back from rolling her eyes.

Striding quickly up the stairs, she snuck into the Sunshine Room. Dakota lay on the window seat, oblivious that anything out of the ordinary was going on. She raised her little head when Nova entered the room.

"I'm so sorry, but I have to." She plucked the kitten from her nap and hurried her to the bathroom, nabbing the quilt of the United States on the way. Nova placed the quilt into the bathtub and tenderly set Dakota on top of it.

"Please, please, PLEASE stay quiet," Nova whispered. Dakota cocked her head, confused.

For good measure, Nova flushed the toilet and washed her hands. She waved goodbye to Dakota and shut the bathroom door completely, barring the room.

By the time she'd made it back to the first floor, Mr. Briar had inspected all the rooms outside of the leprechaun's new lair. Mac was back to bouncing his ball, whistling cheerily while he did so. No doubt a cover-up for the ruckus in the office.

"PHEW. I feel MUCH better." She rubbed her stomach and feigned relief. Mr. Briar chose graciously not to comment.

"Want to check the second floor?" Nova let him go up the stairs first so she could keep an eye on him and redirect when necessary. He squinted into Mr. Russell's room, absorbing the unmade bed and dusty nooks and crannies, jotting all of it down in his notes. Nova was happy to take him into the Sunshine Room, as it remained her favorite room in the house. Mr.

Briar was pleased she was keeping it clean and being attentive in caring for the space. That bit made it into his notebook as well.

He gave the bathroom door a wide berth, and Nova internally rejoiced. She thought they were in the clear until they reached the base of the attic stairs.

"I do believe I missed this room the last time." He creaked clumsily up the steps.

"Ohhhhh, that's just storage. Nothing exciting up there."

There may not have been anything incriminating in the attic, but for some reason she felt defensive of the room. It wasn't meant to be a public gathering ground.

Against her pleas, Mr. Briar yanked on the drawstring for the bulb. He did not step up into the attic, but instead, merely glanced around from the top step, before shutting the light off again. He didn't even make a note of it, which stunned Nova. She couldn't fathom why it hadn't struck him as an important room.

When they'd made it back downstairs, Mr. Briar gave Mac a nod of the head which translated to an introvert's version of 'goodbye'. Nova nearly fist pumped when he exited the house. Crisis averted.

His tour of the outside was remarkably short. Knowing Mr. Briar's admiration of schedules, Nova was sure he wanted to get back on the road. When he finally shuffled back to his car to tell her farewell, she was so relieved that she threw her arms around Mr. Briar's round basketball middle and gave him a gentle squeeze. She could tell he was stunned by the way he patted her on the head, responding with a gentle

"Take care". Her face turned red as a strawberry when she realized in all the time she'd known him, she had never once hugged Mr. Briar. If she was going for inconspicuous, she had failed miserably.

"Would you let Mr. Russell know that I will be giving him a call either today or tomorrow? It is not typical for the caretaker to be absent from these meetings." His tone softened. "But it is good to see you doing well, Nova. Let me know if you need anything before my next drop in."

Nova gave him a half-hearted wave and took a few steps back from the car. When the clunker was nothing more than a speck of metal in the sea of endless green, Nova threw up both her arms in triumph, whooping and dancing about. All things considered, as hard as it was for her to admit it, this had been a pretty fantastic day. There were so many ways the dam could have broken, but instead they had actually salvaged the situation. Nova would have to think of a way to repay Mac for his loyalty.

Sometime during her celebratory dance, another dot appeared on the horizon, moving down the road at a chug-along pace. Because traffic was minimal in the middle of nowhere, Nova became instantly alert.

"No, no, no, no, no," she repeated over and over, as if the chant could change anything.

She and Mac had survived sneaking into the attic, bringing a leprechaun to life, trapping said leprechaun against its will, and a surprise home visit from Mr. Briar. For all their achievement, Nova found herself stymied in the driveway, watching Mr. Russell driving toward the house and her brain completely flummoxed. There was no reasonable excuse in the world to explain away a rogue leprechaun destroying his office. She didn't think even Mac was smooth enough to cover the incident up. She thought they would have a couple of hours to fix the chaotic aftermath.

Leaping into action, she sprinted into the house to make the most of the remaining minute, though it was likely in vain.

Chapter Thirty

Do the Time

Nova spent her last available minute considering the risk of entering the office and trying to capture the leprechaun. Even if they managed to whisk him away before Mr. Russell got into the house, they would still have an extraordinary mess to address.

Mac pushed the door the slightest bit ajar so Nova could assess the damage. It was not a pretty sight. The only object left standing in the room was the large wooden desk. The floor was so littered with books and debris it seemed as if a hideous carpet of garbage was covering the hardwood. The lamp had been responsible for the crashing sound, and shards of glass sprinkled the mess like confetti. A potted plant that Nova hadn't even known existed had been upended from its dirt and turned upside down, roots reaching to the ceiling in a garish sort of way, like a desperate hand. Almost all of the bookshelves were disheveled, and it was safe to say that a good half of Mr. Russell's literature collection had been properly destroyed. Ripped pages were strewn about everywhere, some shredded so terribly they resembled the grass you'd find at the bottom of an Easter basket. The leprechaun sat proudly atop the ceiling fan, surveying his work with a smug expression. What an imp. After only a second, Nova closed the door. The jig was up.

"Maybe we could..." Mac trailed away, catching Nova's furtive stare and knowing it was hopeless.

She cleared her throat and took his hand, far too touchy feely for her own liking, but she owed him a debt of gratitude that lodged a sizable lump in her throat.

"You didn't have to help me today... and you don't have to stay now. I appreciate all you've done, but... this isn't going to end well. I would understand if you wanted to leave before he gets home."

Mac tapped at his cheek with his other hand as if he was pondering her offer. She could have cried when he broke out his toothy grin and gave her hand an amiable squeeze. A wave of relief washed over her as she understood she wouldn't have to face this obstacle alone. It was a novel feeling, the feeling of belonging.

"Don't do the crime if ya can't do the time." Mac's tone of voice was cheery as ever. Nova curiously wondered how he managed to stay so positive, especially in circumstances this dire. She'd have to ask him later, as the screen door was swinging open in that instant, and Mr. Russell arrived home.

His gaze was sharp and lucid, something Nova was both thankful for and wary of. He had caught them in a personal moment, their hands clasped together like friends sharing a secret. Nova immediately released Mac's grip and took a deep breath to prepare herself.

As if on cue, the noise in the office returned. The leprechaun must have grown bored and returned to the portion of literature he had previously left untouched. Nova gritted her teeth and tried to ignore the commotion.

Mr. Russell took a step forward, instantly intrigued.

"Amigo?" he asked imploringly.

Nova shook her head, frozen to the spot. Precisely then, like clockwork, they heard a scratching sound against the screen door, along with some pitiful whining. Mr. Russell opened the door for Amigo. He entered the house with his tail tucked between his legs and his head low to the ground, sniffing for a threat. He had clearly taken the leprechaun's assault personally. Mr. Russell patted him, unawares, and took another guess.

"...Dakota?"

Mac went to nod, but Nova stopped him. Her head turned side to side again, and those tears from earlier threatened to spill over.

Mr. Russell pursed his lips and strode to the base of the stairs, peering upwards toward the attic. He seemed to guess where this was going before they even said a word. Nova dared not turn to face him.

"How long ago did you use the easel?" His voice was simmering, quiet. Not angry, per se, but distinctly disappointed.

Nova had trouble finding her voice. Thankfully, Mac stepped in and replied.

"A couple of hours ago, sir. I asked Nova to teach me how to paint, kind of pressured her, if I'm being honest." This wasn't Mac's first rodeo.

Mr. Russell studied them both for a moment more and then waved them to the table to sit down. The chaos in the office continued, and it was all Nova could do not to cringe at the uproar.

Once they were seated, it was Mr. Russell's turn for a deep breath. He gathered his thoughts and then, surprisingly even keel, addressed them very directly, looking both of them straight in the eye.

"I never explicitly told you that you couldn't use the easel," he began. Nova listened in a daze, cautiously hopeful this may turn out better than she had anticipated.

"However, I would have preferred you to ask permission before using my materials." Her stomach felt nauseous.

"Mac, I'm not sure what your plans are tomorrow, but if you're willing, I'm imagining the office is going to need to be tidied up in the morning."

Mac's reply was short and simple. "I'll be here."

"I think it best if you head home for now."

Mac was out of his chair in a wink, and Nova couldn't fault him. She probably would have left before Mr. Russell had even gotten home. As he trod to the door, Mac turned and gave her a small wave. She tried to smile but couldn't bring herself to wave back. The room was painfully quiet after he vanished from view, an unnerving calm before a storm. Well, outside of the obnoxious, ear-splitting leprechaun antics.

Mr. Russell let her sit for a good amount of time stewing in her worry, and not really knowing what to say. She played with a strand of her hair because her hands couldn't keep still. She was determined not to talk first.

"You'll need to start the morning very early tomorrow. I would prefer the office to be clean before we have to leave."

Nova started at that and tossed her head up to protest. He couldn't take her back to the group home now. She'd never be able to escape from there.

"Leave?" she sputtered, blubbering like a fish out of water. "I know I used the attic without permission, but I promise I'll clean the office from top to bottom. I just don't know how we're going to get the… art… out of there."

"You used the easel this morning, right?"

Nova didn't like saying it out loud. "We did."

"Then it won't be a problem tomorrow." His voice was monotone, and she couldn't read his emotions at all.

"Please," was all she could think to say.

Mr. Russell got flustered. "I know you prefer your alone time, but I can't very well leave you here all day after what's happened. I've got a job tomorrow, and you're going to have to come along and help me."

A job. He wasn't taking her back to the group home. He was bringing her to work. Instantaneously, the room seemed brighter, the birds outside were chirping happily, and Nova felt so light she could have floated off her chair. He wasn't abandoning her, even though she had gone behind his back. How was that possible?

The joy must have shown on her face, because Mr. Russell got formal all of a sudden.

"I do, however, think you should spend the rest of the day in your room, contemplating the choices you made today. I'll bring you up some dinner in a bit." His voice was firm, but not at all confident. The Dad approach was new to him.

She pointed to the door, not wanting to start a new argument but concerned about the predicament.

"Is there anything I should do to… bar the door?" she asked studiously.

Mr. Russell took it for stalling.

"I'll keep an eye on the door. Like I said, it won't be a problem in the morning."

Nova had to keep herself from skipping to the stairs, blatantly relieved to have dodged the bullet of 'return to sender'. A thought struck her before she left the kitchen, and she turned around.

"Ummmm… while you were out, Mr. Briar stopped by for a visit."

Mr. Russell's eyes got big as saucers, his shoulders stiffened, and he looked extremely uncomfortable.

"Did he? And he toured the house? What all did he find?" Mr. Russell was immediately on edge. The prospect of an outsider discovering his secret bothered him. Nova didn't know whether to feel flattered or entertained.

"Nothing of importance," she reassured him. "Mac helped me with that."

Trudging up the stairs, she knowingly declared, "He said he would call you today or tomorrow. You know, just to check in."

Now they both had something to mull on late into the night.

28 de Octubre de 1991

Dear Van Gogh,

What a time to be alive! Does the sarcasm translate? This week, we've been preparing to celebrate Dia de los Muertos... the Day of the Dead. As a child, it was easy for me to overlook the sadness of the holiday, mostly because I was excited my relatives would join us in spirit for the festivities. I always thought I could see them out of the corner of my eye, like little fireflies in the night. Unfortunately, as I've gotten older, I have also matured... become wiser. We aren't supposed to feel sad when we lose those we love, but I'm finding that more often than not, I feel out of sorts... if not for the people I've already lost, then for the future that won't ever be mine.

Day of the Dead is a time to honor our family and friends who have passed on. My family creates a decorative altar where we place candles and pictures of our loved ones. I was struck by the idea to ask my father if I could build a handmade altar this year. He didn't entertain my plan for even a moment. Instead, my father and Tio will make the new altar we need, as I sit idly by. Will my entire life be spent watching from the sidelines? I don't mean to sound morbid, but it's difficult to stay upbeat in my current frame of mind.

I'm sorry to hear your schooling has been stressing you lately. It's exciting that you are graduating at the end of this semester. I know your future feels uncertain, but it's amazing you can make it whatever you want. Art may not be the most typical career path, but I have faith with your ability, the world will be yours for the taking. You have no idea how envious I am of that. No matter what happens, know that your penpal will always be around to keep you on track. Continue writing... it's the only thing keeping me sane!

Sincerely,
Mari

Chapter Thirty-One

Ettenborough

Nova had predicted the cleaning project would be an insurmountable task, but the morning exceeded her expectations. When she crept into the office at dawn, under the direct supervision of Mr. Russell, the leprechaun was nowhere to be found. His legacy, however, was the most intimidating mess she had ever laid eyes on.

Thankfully, the leprechaun left about a third of the books untouched. The only good news. Nova was disheartened at all of the stories that had been lost, the pages scattered about and shredded in such a careless way. She shuffled her feet through the mess with a soft shhhh-shhhhh-shhhhhh. The hooligan had hung some of the paper willy-nilly off the ceiling as if it were raining Dickens. The floor was a trash dump, debris collected into mountains and valleys of tangled clutter. Nova only made it a few steps before her path was completely blocked. The wreckage was astronomical. She felt a new sting when she realized Mr. Russell's desk chair had been dismantled and flung about the room. She covered her eyes with her hands, not wanting to look any more.

Mr. Russell didn't know what to say at first. He just stood in the doorway, massaging his chin, crestfallen and bedraggled from a night with little sleep. A knock from the front door brought him to; he lumbered over to allow Mac entrance to the party.

"I'll go ahead and get a roll of trash bags." Mr. Russell intoned. He was lost in thought, and visibly discouraged, with his shoulders stiff around his neck.

"I think we'll need them," Mac's quip was untimely, and Nova moved her hands to cover her ears. Somehow, she was going to have to find a way to make this right with Mr. Russell. The damage to the office wasn't just aesthetic. Many of his valuable possessions had been turned into pulp.

Dakota was the only individual on the scene gathering any enjoyment. She leapt into the room as soon as the door opened, diving gracefully into the mounds of tattered paper. She surfaced again like she was doing the backstroke in a pool, batting at the remnants of the cherished books with her paws. Amigo let out a grumpy bark, disapproving of the childish antics.

It took Mac and Nova the better part of the morning to make a dent in the disarray. They filled ten huge, black trash bags, and only managed to clear half the room. Both were droopy and sore with fatigue when Mr. Russell gave them the go ahead to take a break. Mac and Nova guzzled down their glasses of water after they had removed the garden gloves Mr. Russell had loaned them. It was better than picking up the trash with their hands.

"Unfortunately, Mac, Nova and I have a commitment this afternoon. The rest of the office will have to wait until another day. I appreciate the effort you put forth this morning." Was that a hint of pride in his voice? Mr. Russell even held out his hand for a quick shake. Nova tried to keep herself from being envious. Her work day had only just begun.

"It was my pleasure, sir. Let me know when we can finish the job, and I'll be here. Sorry again about... everything." His giant exhale rustled his bangs. Mac may have been genuine in his apology, but his foot was already halfway through the door, resting on the porch. He was more than ready to depart.

After he left, Mr. Russell gave Nova an oversized gray t-shirt that was large enough for a grown man.

"You'll want to wear an old pair of pants too. We will inevitably be ruining some clothes after lunch." The comment was foreboding, and Nova's body slouched as if she carried a barbell on her shoulders. She didn't know how she could handle another grueling shift, but she would have to try. She owed Mr. Russell that much.

After she changed, Nova and Mr. Russell packed the painting supplies into the bed of his truck. Big buckets of paint, drop cloths, rollers, brushes, and even a paint spray gun. Mr. Russell whistled the tune of Camptown Races. Nova kept quiet and fought the urge to flee.

Once the bed of the truck was stocked, Mr. Russell directed it up the road, heading toward the fork. The summer heat was heavy but dulled by the puffy white clouds drifting through the sky. Nova was grateful the temperature was lower than it had been the previous day, especially if they were going to be spending time outside. As they pulled into the parking lot of Ellie's Place, Nova noticed a vast array of cloud animals flouncing through the heavens: a puffy elephant, trunk raised, winked at her as it passed by, a lone white wolf howled to the non-existent moon, and a shaggy cumulous dog wagged its happy tail, suspiciously similar to Amigo begging for some play time. She opted to stay in the truck and watch the parade while Mr. Russell retrieved their take-out lunch. She was not in a conversational mood as he stowed the containers on the dash.

By the time the truck was chugging up the opposite side of the fork, Nova had fallen asleep against the headrest, mouth wide open and snoring. He let her rest that way for much of the journey. She only jolted awake when the truck hiccupped over a pronounced speed bump. Swiping the drool discreetly from her chin, Nova pretended as if the nap hadn't happened at all. When her vision cleared, she sat straight up in her seat, interested in the change of scenery.

Mr. Russell piloted them down a dated Main Street, with old rickety buildings situated on either side of the avenue that waved at her in greeting.

The gravel was gone, and the street consisted of a collection of muted red bricks laid in symmetrical rows. Everywhere she looked there was old world character. Antique storefronts leaned into each other like familiar friends, smiling at Nova as she passed them by. Colorful awnings decorated the windows, and hand painted lettering arched across the glass in a display of allure, beckoning her to enter and explore. She saw a patriotic barber shop decked out in red, white, and blue; an ancient bowling alley where memory conjured the impressive crash of pins with a well-placed strike; a humble grocer's market with delicious fruits and veggies stacked generously outside the door, and a lopsided library, front doors swung open like the pages of a book. Nova's interest piqued when she noticed the fanciful ice cream parlor, white columns with spires and flags providing the framework for the door. Now was not the time to beg Mr. Russell for ice cream, but the storefront was so inviting she found herself licking her lips. She could taste the minty sweet treat on her tongue. She thought they were removed from civilization, but in truth, while this town was ancient, it was undeniably charming.

"Where are we?" Nova queried, slurring her words, groggy from sleep.

"Ettenborough." Mr. Russell said matter-of-factly.

That's a mouthful. Nova wished dearly to explore the nooks and crannies of this newly discovered place. Upon quick examination, it may appear to the passer-by to be the same as any small country town: stop signs instead of lights and the downtown stretch being less than a mile. After having been isolated at the farmhouse with only fields around, the town was a feast to Nova's eyes, a spectacular banana split sundae with extra chocolate sauce and sprinkles.

Once they left the buildings behind, Mr. Russell took a left and arrived at a bland, unimpressive spot. Sprawling across the expansive lawn was a long, angular low building with a dark roof and tan brick walls. Oak trees guarded the perimeter of the building, and a vast collection of windows punctuated the sides. A handcrafted sign next to the double door in front read 'Ettenborough Public School'. The most fascinating vista lay round the back of the school; she could just discern monkey bars and a bright red slide swerving toward a fantastical playground. The parking lot was blacktop with no lines to speak of, but there were no other cars around, so they pulled close to the building.

Mr. Russell handed Nova a styrofoam container that smelled divine. She opened it to reveal a freshly made grilled cheese sandwich, with thick slices of toast and ooey-gooey cheese. Ms. Ellie had outdone herself, and Nova's stomach flip-flopped hungrily as she took an enormous first bite. Mr. Russell had ordered the same, and they enjoyed their lunch in pleasant silence. Nova inched down her window to allow a landscape-laced breeze; pine needles, hay stacks, and fresh cut grass tickled her nostrils as the country wrapped her in a warm summer hug. Maybe there was more to Ettenborough than her first glance. Maybe the town wanted to know her too and was reaching out in the only way it knew how.

Chapter Thirty-Two

Restored

When Nova slid out of the truck and jumped to the ground after they had finished their scrumptious lunch, the puffy white cloud animals tumbled about with the wind in a joyful circus act. Aside from igniting her imagination, they provided valuable shade and made the summertime heat bearable. Mr. Russell accessed the truck bed and carried the bulk of the supplies closer to the school. It took him three or four trips, and Nova squirmed next to the truck's tailgate, not knowing what to do or say. Steeling herself for the upcoming job, she finally fished a few lone brushes from the back of the truck, feeling rather useless, and followed.

Up close, the school was wrinkled in both the siding and foundation, its age evident in its tired sag and the massive metal window latches of yesteryear. A great effort had been put forth to counteract the effect of time through various, obvious patch jobs. But it was sorely in need of some spit and polish. That, she guessed, is where Mr. Russell came into play.

Mr. Russell moved deftly at his job, opening the paint buckets and blending the contents with a stirrer to mix them evenly. With his baggy clothes and haphazard hair, he resembled an artsy wizard stirring a thick, mysterious potion. He was courteous enough to explain the painting process to Nova as he prepped. She found herself fascinated by the differences between small and large scale painting.

"Ordinarily for speed, you could use the spray gun to paint." He held the artistic weapon in his hands, brandishing it with enthusiasm and striking a pose. "For jobs that require more TLC, I prefer good old-fashioned paint brushes and rollers. We'll be painting the brick exterior."

He poured the paint into a couple of paint trays, and Nova was elated to see it was a pale, delicate green, comparable to the color of mint chocolate chip ice cream. She tried to envision the school swathed in the hue, and thought definitively it would be a vast improvement.

Mr. Russell showed her how to hold the roller in a way conducive to painting and then they were off to the races. He laid drop cloths over the grass to curb the spatter, a smart move since Nova sprayed gobs of paint across her t-shirt with the first few rotations of her roller. She refocused, hyper alert, trying her hardest to get all of her paint from the tray to the side of the building, but didn't know how to move fast enough to keep it from dripping. She fumbled about until Mr. Russell demonstrated how to roll the excess paint off within the confines of the tray. His instruction made the task a million times easier.

There was a sense of rhythm and restfulness to the job; Nova was thrilled to witness the side of the school transform. Her artist soul rejoiced, and she recognized the wall as a giant blank canvas, ripe for unique creativity. The pressure applied to the roller was therapeutic, and the tension melted from her shoulders, as if she was engaged in a painter's session of yoga.

Mr. Russell handed her a water bottle when they were about halfway through with the side of the building. Nova took a long swig and dumped the remainder over her head with a contagious chortle. Mr. Russell's responding chuckle was hearty and genuine, a deep-throated warble like an amused owl. Picking up their rollers once more, he struck up a conversation.

"My grandfather's responsible for my love of art." The comment was wistful, and a coy smile played about his lips. Nova just listened, feeling lucky he wanted to share a piece of his past with her.

"I actually hated art in school, or maybe I just hated school in general. I tended to daydream instead of paying attention to the teachers." He moved with fluidity, like he was slow-dancing when he painted. Nova was entranced, following his movement with rapt attention.

"I always thought I would grow up to be a basketball star. All the men in my family were tall and I loved the pace of the sport. I practiced all the time with my brothers. I was the youngest, so putting up with their teasing was the price of admission." He chuckled at that. "I thought the more I played basketball, the greater the likelihood I would turn into a star athlete. The unfair truth is I'm an awful shot. They mocked me for it.

"Kids can be hot-headed, and one day I'd had enough of their critiques. I wanted to prove to them basketball was my destiny, and I had what it took to be a pro player. They dared me to sink a ball and hold the rim. I was far too small to reach the rim on my own, so I climbed to the top of our shed and tried to make the jump from there."

Nova winced, knowing what was coming.

"I spent the rest of my summer stranded in the house with a broken leg. I was lucky enough that our grandfather lived with us at the time. He shook me out of my funk and inspired me to give art a try. I was open to it because I was so bored. I learned channeling art as a creative escape meant more to me than the endless basketball drills."

Mr. Russell set down his roller and refilled their paint trays, never missing a beat.

"I loved coaxing a picture out of nothing. Turns out all the time I'd spent daydreaming in school was training me to be an artist. My grandfather passed away the following year, and I still believe that summer with him is one of my fondest memories. I owe him my identity."

Nova found herself grinning absentmindedly at Mr. Russell's story. She had never known her biological grandparents but had lived with the odd elderly couple and always appreciated the wisdom they had toward life. Her own introduction to art had happened differently.

Mr. Russell suddenly grew serious, his voice quiet, but friendly.

"I remember what it was like to be a child who loved art. Once I became more confident, the supplies were magic to me. I could make my own world and be the master of it all. I see a lot of that spark in you. And I guess what I'm trying to say is… I understand what drew you to the easel. I can forgive you for using it. I just hope you feel you can come to me the next time you have a question or request."

Nova felt a warmth seep into the pit of her stomach that had nothing to do with the weather. She nodded at him and continued painting with a restored vigor, her cheeks turning pink. The indiscretion yesterday wasn't the end of their relationship.

She wasn't sure what exactly brought her guard down; if it was Mr. Russell's openness or just her relief that she wasn't going back to the group home. Regardless, when he opened up to her about his childhood, she felt the inclination to do the same.

"I've lived in more houses than I can count. Some of them were nice, some not." She kept her eyes trained on her work, forcibly trying to keep the conversation moving forward, fighting against her basic instinct to clam up.

"I wasn't always into art either, and I never spent enough time in school to really decide in class if it was something I was good at."

She paused, preparing herself to step off the edge of the precipice into unchartered territory.

"The longest I spent with a family was six months. They lived near the ocean and had a house with a view of the beach. Everything in the house was pristine, so I felt out of place when I got there. The parents seemed welcoming, but I got the feeling from them that I wasn't supposed to touch anything. I didn't really care though, because their daughter, Emily, became my very best friend.

"Emily's family was well-off, and she had her own art alcove at the back of her room. The paints, pencils, markers, and glitter made me dizzy... there was so much to see. Emily and I would spend hours working on projects together. She taught me the basics of art, how to start with a simple shape and then morph it into something more. She was a great teacher, and always shared with me. I was nine at the time."

Nova tried to ignore the warning in her head telling her to stop... that getting too personal was dangerous.

"Emily's parents had high hopes for her. She attended a private school and was talented at pretty much everything. Because she was so interested in art, her parents signed her up for professional classes. Emily only agreed to go if I could go too. I never understood why she was so stubborn about it, but she was always saying she thought my drawings were special."

The words came faster now, in an avalanche, as if holding back the story for so many years had built up a pressure inside of her.

"Taking those classes was the beginning of the end for us. We would go twice a week and learn all kinds of drawing techniques. The instructors showed us how to create depth in pencil artwork with shading, and how to follow any hunches we may have when drawing. It became more and more natural for me... to the point where I imagined the pencil was telling me where it wanted to move. I started drawing everywhere I went. Emily always encouraged me. She even let me have one of her notebooks to practice."

Nova set her roller down and leaned back against the unpainted wall, suddenly feeling faint, a hand over her heart.

"It was spring when the class concluded with an art show. We all got little diplomas and pats on the back. It was cheesy, but one of my happiest moments ever. Emily held my hand while the families clapped for the students. After the show, the instructors pulled Emily's parents to the side. They were across the room, but I was close enough to watch. Her parents thought Emily was the best artist in class. If you had asked me, I would have agreed. But as her parents talked to the instructors, their faces changed from proud to upset."

Nova took a shaky breath, finding it difficult to materialize the memory. Now that she had started, it had to be finished, like a doodle calling out to her.

"The teachers told her parents they wanted to offer me a position at an art academy over the summer.

I was shocked. Emily's parents got upset that I was as good, possibly better, at art than their daughter. The art academy had been their dream for her. For as nice as Emily was to me, even she couldn't convince them to let me stay. It took less than a day for them to call Mr. Briar to come pick me up. Emily drew me a picture with her colored pencils and was the only one to wave goodbye when we drove away. I couldn't wave back, couldn't even move. I didn't think I would ever see her again. It made me angry."

Nova's voice died down to a whisper. She felt hollow inside, as if there was a great cavern of emptiness residing in her chest. An Emily-shaped hole. The bugs continued to buzz and flit about as if the world wasn't crashing down around them. Nova hung her head and dropped to the ground, hiding her face in her elbow and trying to quell the trauma and sadness of her past. She didn't feel strong enough.

Mr. Russell said nothing. Instead, he sat next to her and rested his hand on her shoulder. In that moment, some weight of the memory transferred from her to him, and she started to cry, as if he had flipped some sort of switch. They stayed immobile, in quiet coexistence, as long as it took for the tears to run dry.

6 de Diciembre de 1991

Dear Van Gogh,

Every day that passes, I feel more and more distant from this place. My family hasn't noticed. I'm getting good at going through the daily routine without making much of a fuss. I help my Mama and Papa at the market, stocking shelves and assisting customers, bored out of my mind. I spend my days thinking of you and how bright your future is. I find I want to chase my own dreams, though I know it would mean severing ties with my family. Is it worth that cost?

You're nearing the end of your school year. Are you ready to graduate and join the ranks of the employed? What are your plans for after college?

When you become famous, will you remember me?

If I'm being honest, my correspondence with you gives me great joy... perhaps my only joy, since the tasks I once thrilled in have been banned. My hands are physically sore in the absence of my tools. My father hid them away when I confronted him about the altar. I know he loves me, but he wants me to have a secure life, and he believes I must marry and be only a housewife, or work forever for the family business. What he considers security feels like a death sentence to me. I can feel my dreams withering away like an unwatered plant. You are the only sustenance I have left.

I've been toying with the idea of taking a trip in the coming months. Our time together here was a chance for me to show you my world. Now I want to see yours. Write to me and tell me if you think that is a possibility... if you could be the place I run to. My desperation is making me long-winded, but please know every word I speak is true. I will wait for your reply and hold tight to the last of my dreams.

Sincerely Yours,
Mari

Chapter Thirty-Three

Fragrance and Bubbles

Mr. Russell and Nova completed only one of the walls before the sun sunk low in the sky. He had allowed her some quiet time with her thoughts as she recovered from sharing her story. Nova was drained, but also more lightweight, as if a burden had been lifted off her shoulders.

When it became too dark to work, they loaded the truck in unison and set out toward home. The lights along Main Street were blazing in the dusky darkness. The storefronts were illuminated from within, creating the illusion that she was studying a series of paintings in a museum. The interior of the businesses were still and empty, but Nova enjoyed pretending she was window shopping. She wondered if Mr. Russell had ever spent any time perusing the shops or if he would consider taking her someday. Gazing down at her floppy t-shirt, covered in paint, she knew now was not the time.

A short while later, when Mr. Russell guided the truck into the driveway, he shut off the ignition and turned to face her. Nova stiffened, hoping he wouldn't bring up her past again. She wanted to spend the night focusing only on the present.

"I'm going to put together some dinner after I change clothes." Mr. Russell was comfortable and at ease. He twirled his keys on his pointer finger as he spoke.

"If you'd like, you could take a bath in the meantime. The bubble bath and towels are in the bathroom closet. I'd say you've earned it after all the hard work you put in today." He paused.

"I'm proud of your help. You really are a natural painter. You'd better be careful or I may hire you as a permanent member of the team." He laughed at his own joke and exited the truck.

Nova's cheeks flushed at his compliment. Despite what she thought that morning, she actually liked painting the school. Adding her touch to the building made her feel like a piece of her belonged in Ettenborough... like she had made a small difference in improving the town. Maybe she would ask Mr. Russell if she could help finish the job.

Her muscles ached from overexertion as she climbed to the second floor, snagging a pair of pajamas from her room and making her way to the bathroom. She turned the brass knob for the tub with a squeak, and a stream of water cascaded out of the faucet. Checking the temperature to be lukewarm, Nova proceeded to the closet with a twirl, genuinely excited for her bath. The door opened with a loud creak, and she got a face full of musty, storage smell. Coughing into her shoulder, Nova thrust her arm in the linen closet to retrieve a fluffy gray towel. The bubble bath was just out of her reach, situated on the second shelf from the top. Nova jumped as high as she could, but her fingers only grazed the bottle. Checking the sturdiness of the bottom shelf, she gingerly placed her feet on it to gain some height.

Stretching with all her might, she pulled the bubble bath victoriously off the shelf. As she did so, a glint of glass seized her attention. From her position standing on her makeshift stool, she could just see to the furthest part of the ledge, the portion of shelf hidden in shadow. A thick layer of dust coated the surface, interspersed with little objects and knick-knacks that flashed like pennies in a wishing well. There were crystal flower vases, shiny picture frames, delicate porcelain figurines, and one of those classic perfume bottles with the little squeezy puff ball to dispense the fragrance.

Curious, Nova sniffed at the perfume bottle, but didn't catch a whiff of anything. Giving the ball a soft squeeze, a cloud of aroma dispersed around her face, again making her hack from the displaced dust. She almost lost her footing but righted herself at the last second. What was that smell? It seemed so familiar. Intoxicating and fragrant… wildflowers?

Shaking her head to clear her nose, Nova puzzled over why she recognized the scent. Maybe Mr. Russell had a garden where she'd registered it before. It drove her crazy that she couldn't place where she'd experienced the smell.

Lurching back to reality, Nova's bath had filled to the rim of the tub, and was about to transform the bathroom into an indoor swimming pool. She hurriedly shut off the water and drained a little of it before adding her sudsy bubbles, having to churn the bath with her hands to create an iridescent froth. *Next time, bubbles go in first.* She frowned as splashes of water heaved over the side of the tub and sprinkled across the floor. Discarding her paint laden clothes into a messy heap, Nova lowered herself with a sigh into the warm water. She closed her eyes and relished the wave of relaxation that embraced her. The knick-knacks in the closet were the newest addition to the lengthy list of mysteries she had discovered in this house. Why didn't Mr. Russell set the objects out as decoration? Pretty trinkets would substantially help the farmhouse's interior design, or lack thereof.

The collection of trinkets reminded her of her own secret treasure trove under her bed. She would never admit it, but she was more sentimental than she let on. Nova had taken something trivial from every home that had been good to her. A rock, a quarter, a leaf… she'd tried to pick items with the least amount of monetary value, so it didn't feel like stealing. The pieces she'd saved made her feel as if she had a history and helped her to remember the journey she'd been on throughout her life. The picture from Emily of the rainbow butterfly was her most recent takeaway, and it had been a gift. She hadn't stayed anywhere since that was worthy of remembering.

Maybe Mr. Russell kept those objects tucked away because they were so meaningful to him. Maybe, like her treasures, it caused him pain to look at them all the time, but he wanted to know they were safe.

Nova bolted upright in the bath, hit by a sudden spark of understanding; the water splashed against the wall like a splotch of clear paint. The aroma, from the perfume bottle, she recalled where she had smelled it before. It had been hidden away in the Sunshine Room… and wafted off the paper letters from her end table. Which meant whoever had written the letters was of some relation to Mr. Russell, and that whoever it was had been important to him. Was there more to Mr. Russell than met the eye? Had he loved and lost someone too? Nova dropped back into the bath, putting her head all the way under the water, blowing bubbles out her nose and trying to temper the theories gurgling in her mind.

2 de Agosto de 1992

Dearest Van Gogh,

So much has changed in the last year. Your letters carried me through the most difficult time of my life, and I thought today, our wedding day, would be cause for settling the score.

You have never denied me my dreams or desires. When I showed up on your doorstep at the beginning of the year, you welcomed me with open arms. Without the approval or support of my family, your kindness made all the difference. I have seen more of the world in the past six months than I ever imagined I would, and I owe all of those experiences to you. Our relationship was rooted in friendship and has blossomed into the most beautiful garden I have ever seen. Who would I be without you next to me? It is with an overflowing heart that I face you today and speak my vows, pledging my forever to you.

I foresee a future of laughter, love, surprises, and daily adventure. I have always wanted the wings to soar, but you have taught me that home is not a cage... that to have a place to call my own is as important as traversing the world. I can't wait to build our own world together. I love you. You are the artist of my soul.

Love always,
Your Mari

Chapter Thirty-Four

Miracle

Nova slept like a rock, and luckily, Mr. Russell let her. She was unconscious well into the afternoon, the previous day's escapades having exhausted her completely. When she did wake, she was disoriented, and lay still for a few minutes in bed to regain her bearings. The birds were singing a happy tune outside her window. The sunlight fell in shards upon the floor, morphing the Sunshine Room into a kaleidoscope of light. She stretched her arms far above her head as her joints popped and felt a distinct sense of contentment envelop her. As achy as her body remained after all the manual labor, Nova was grateful for it. She had accomplished something significant, and the pride glowed within her like a new light bulb.

Nova padded down the stairs groggily, planning to eat a quick breakfast of solitude, but was surprised to find Mr. Russell seated at the kitchen table. She presumed he would be working again today. Even more startling was how her cheerful attitude magnified when she realized she was not alone. Nova had always considered herself a lone wolf, a solitary introvert and most comfortable on her own. Yet here she was relieved to have Mr. Russell's company. It was all very confusing.

"Morning, sunshine," Mr. Russell quipped. Nova knew it was a joke directed at her disheveled appearance, but she liked the way the nickname sounded just the same. She tossed him a tired grin.

As Nova poured herself a bowl of cereal, Mr. Russell outlined his plans for the day.

"I wanted to show my appreciation for your help yesterday, so I figured I'd take the day off and assist you in tidying up the office."

Nova's heart skipped a beat, remembering the giant mess she was still expected to clean. Her muscles groaned in protest. She wanted to object but decided to bite her tongue and take the punishment. At least Mr. Russell lending a hand would make the process go faster.

Nova flopped into an open chair and crunched her sweet cereal, savoring the taste of cinnamon in each spoonful. Mr. Russell waited for her objection to finishing the office today. He leaned forward in his chair listening intently. She just munched on her breakfast. After about a minute, he reclined again looking pleased.

"I also thought, should we complete the cleaning in good time, I might teach you about the easel today. You know... if you're interested."

Nova blinked a message in Morse code at this new development. When reality finally hit her, she bounced to her feet, quivering with excitement. At her response, Mr. Russell smiled even wider.

"Are you serious?" she remarked in a breathy whisper. "That would be AMAZING."

Immediately wide awake and raring to go, Nova spooned the rest of her cereal hurriedly into her mouth and raced up the stairs to change. She met Mr. Russell in the office less than two minutes later, feeling electrified: like someone had plugged her into an outlet. He handed her gloves and a garbage bag, and she attacked the mess wholeheartedly.

Between the two of them, the disarray didn't stand a chance. She was sweating and out of breath by the time the floor was completely clear but had not lost any of her energy. It was all Nova could do to keep herself from hurtling straight into the attic. Mr. Russell beamed at her enthusiasm and offered to take the trash out while she changed and washed up. It was the only encouragement she needed. Like a thoroughbred intent on winning the Kentucky Derby, Nova bounded speedily over Amigo's lazy form in the front hallway. She was changed and positioned in the attic before Mr. Russell even made it back inside.

Dakota was in a personable mood and rubbed up against Nova's shins while she waited. Nova petted her back and delighted in the tiny purr vibrating out of her petite body. Mr. Russell appeared at the top of the stairs, having also changed into a fresh set of clothes. He pulled the light on, the brightness washing over his face, and an air of tranquility crossed his countenance. Nova closed her eyes and let the radiating warmth of the attic engulf her. The playful, invisible breeze skimmed across her cheek in greeting. It was happiness, pure and simple.

Mr. Russell ushered her to sit on the stool by the easel as he proceeded confidently to the chest of supplies. To Nova, he was a different person in this sanctuary. Normally, Mr. Russell came across as someone watching life from the sidelines, observing, but not really participating. It was clear this was his domain—where he felt the most at home. His posture was straight and strong, and his stride long and true. Nova caught a glimpse of him in his most real self. She was honored to have the opportunity and knew something incredible was about to happen.

Amigo entered the attic unnoticed and settled himself in a corner of the room. His watchful attitude softened, and he also appeared relaxed. Enough that Dakota clambered up onto his back as he lounged, stretching her body into a yoga pose before lying down herself.

Mr. Russell procured a small scraper, multiple thin brushes, a towel, and a blank palette from his chest of drawers. Ever so gently, he returned to the chest and pushed the front of a wooden emblem at the very top. A wood panel flipped open to reveal a secret compartment that held another paintbrush, this one jet black.

He carried it reverently over to Nova and allowed her to study its markings. All along the handle were beautiful wooden carvings of flowers and plants. The paintbrush was as sparkling and well-cared for as the easel; not a drop of misplaced paint disturbed its inherent sheen. It was a masterpiece all its own.

Mr. Russell looked at the paintbrush as if it had transported him somewhere else, his eyes glazed over while a bittersweet smile played about his lips. He spoke softly, not wanting to ruin the moment.

"This paintbrush and easel are my most prized possessions. They were gifted to me a long time ago by someone I cared about deeply. Over years of practice, I discovered what they were capable of." Mr. Russell ran his hand through his hair, searching for words.

"I know I don't have to convince you, because you've seen the magic. There are still days where I don't believe it. I'm not sure where it comes from, but I've managed to surmise a set of rules as to how it works."

"The paintbrush represents imagination. It's how we bring our thoughts to life, how we create something out of nothing. The strongest source of creation I've found is love." He stammered when he got to the last word, as if it poked an old bruise. Shaking his head, he continued.

"Art is a form of passion, a visual representation of love. We dig down deep within ourselves to find inspiration, and because of the soul searching involved with it, a piece of ourselves is placed in each and every rendering we design. The paintbrush allows a bit of our souls to be seen."

Mr. Russell pointed to the easel, gleaming in the luminescence of the attic.

"The easel is the home where those creations reside, at least for a little while. It allows us to pull inspiration from inside of us and make it tangible for the world to see. Because of the special nature of this particular easel, it works literally as well as figuratively. The wood that was used to fashion the easel is the same wood I utilized to build the fence around the backyard."

Nova was in awe. "YOU built the fence around the backyard? It's flawless. Where did all the wood come from?"

He paused. "I knew a carpenter." A flash of sadness crossed his features. It was there only briefly and then gone again.

"When I first discovered the magical capabilities of the easel, I was afraid it would draw unwanted attention. The fence is a boundary of sorts, without magic, except the paintings always come to life within it. I originally built it as a way to grant my creations some privacy, and naively thought it would keep them from wreaking havoc on the world. That's proven to be a pipe dream. There's been a LOT of trial and error. Luckily, we don't have too many watchful eyes around here."

Mr. Russell raised his eyebrows at her, and Nova smirked, recalling the leprechaun.

"So, the easel is the source of the magic, and you can use it to manifest what lives in your imagination. It only works with images you've conjured inside of you. For instance, I couldn't paint Amigo sleeping in the attic and expect him to come to life; he already exists. I could paint him, sure, but the magic wouldn't take hold. I think it's how our world keeps balance, though that's just a guess."

Nova was mystified, her whole body buzzing at his explanations, but in a good way.

"I knew you were a true artist, with honest to goodness passion for it, when the leprechaun came to life. Only if you put love into your art can it manifest in the real world."

Lost in thought, Nova blushed and looked away.

"Mac was actually the one to paint the leprechaun. But it makes sense. He's one of the most spirited people I know."

At first, she was sad thinking maybe she didn't have what it took to be a true artist. Her brow furrowed with disappointment. Then she remembered.

"I did paint something that came to life. Before the mistake of the leprechaun. It was how I realized the easel was special."

Retrieving the drawing Emily had made, she handed it to Mr. Russell, hesitating only a moment before allowing him to open it.

"My best friend in the world made me that picture. So, I painted it on the easel. It came to life the next morning and I couldn't believe my eyes."

She worried Mr. Russell would be mad to learn she had used the easel a second time without permission, but he smiled instead.

"Your love brought it to life. You remind me of myself, and I see the potential in you. You are capable of impactful art. A gift to cherish, and to use to create. If you'd let me, I'd like to teach you what I know."

Nova was so joyful she felt she would burst like a popcorn kernel and rebound off the walls in sheer bliss, but instead gave him an enthusiastic nod.

Mr. Russell was a mirror image of her joy. In an instant, she could see the similarities between them, like tiny threads of connection bridging any void of separation. They had grown up in different circumstances and different times, but in this way, they were the same.

Feeling her guard drop another inch, Nova threw her arms around Mr. Russell's waist, giving him a brief, awkward, loving squeeze. He hugged her back and the warm breeze returned, circling them both in approval.

Mr. Russell cleared his throat when the hug ended. Nova felt complete, like her heart had been mended and her chest was no longer a black hole.

"So, lesson number one, a demonstration of sorts. Where is a place you have never been, but would like to go? I was always partial to landscapes, and that's what we'll create today."

"If it's a landscape, will it come to life?" Nova asked, a little concerned by the restrictions of the easel.

"It will if I make it unique from anywhere I've actually seen."

Nova stood on her tiptoes and whispered her idea into his ear. Immediately, Mr. Russell was a man with a plan. He took the plastic palette and pressed a healthy variety of paints along its edge. Nova moved off the stool so he could sit, her gut telling her she was about to be impressed.

Mr. Russell entered into a kind of trance, eyes glued to the canvas, paintbrush poised like the sword of a knight. He took a deep breath before plunging into the job, his strokes deliberate and masterful. He knew where each line belonged as if they had previously existed there; the way he mixed colors filled Nova with wonder. He'd only chosen enough colors to fit on the palette, but somehow managed to create a hundred more. He tackled the sky of the painting first, rendering clouds into existence. After he'd completed the background, he began shaping the rest. It was like watching a theatrical show. Nova couldn't peel her eyes away.

Much to her dismay, Mr. Russell stopped to turn and face her. She itched to see the completed picture.

"Aren't you going to finish it?"

"I am, but I think you need a change of scenery first."

Fishing a key from his pocket, he led Nova down to the first floor and over to the back door. A series of clicks emitted from the locks as he worked his way down, each more resounding than the last, like an orchestra building to a crescendo. Nova half expected to be met with thunderous applause when the door opened.

The backyard was plain and utterly normal, composed of a large grass lawn and a cluster of trees at the far left side, with most of the outside landscape hidden behind the wooden fence. From her location on the elevated wooden deck, she could see the pond, like an infinity pool, over the top of the fence.

"I want you to see it happen." Mr. Russell stated matter-of-factly. Nova sat down on the top step of the deck, compliant and excited, her hands squeezed together as if in prayer. Mr. Russell returned to the attic. She waited.

She couldn't say if ten minutes had passed or an hour when the fog started rolling in from the pond. Great ivory clouds amassed on the water and billowed over the fence like a speed bump, spreading in a tidal wave across the lawn. The entire expanse of land turned to a cloudy white, identical to the canvas resting inside the attic. Ever so softly, the fog illuminated from the inside and shapes began to emerge. Nova watched, shell-shocked on the deck, tears rolling openly down her face, the luckiest girl in the entire world. Never before had she witnessed a miracle. Never again would she be the same.

18 de Febrero de 1999

Dearest Van Gogh,

This letter was recommended by my therapist and is my attempt to sort through the emotions waging war inside of me. The line between what's possible and impossible has blurred, and my heart has shattered in its wake. I feel like I'm transforming into an empty shell, hollow and scarred on the inside... damaged goods.

I have always wanted a child. You know as much. We have been honest with each other in our marriage, and now I must be honest again. The news from the doctor has devastated me. I don't know how to open my eyes in the morning without feeling lost. My hope to carry your baby has vanished, and it's as if my body betrayed me.

I never imagined a world where having a child of our own would be impossible. It's a reality I must come to terms with. Please be patient with me as I grieve. I love you more than words can say, but a piece of my heart will always belong to the baby that can't be. I must deal with mourning in my own way. Take my hand and lead me away from this sadness.

Love always,
Your Mari

Chapter Thirty-Five

Jungle Trek

Nova waited on the step, frozen, anticipating Mr. Russell would join her soon. Shapes emerged from the fog, gradually coming into view as if the lens of a camera was gaining focus. Her dream world was being born right before her eyes.

Tall, exotic trees with strange leaves appeared in the mist, vines draped across their branches like massive snakes; bold flowers of every possible color accented the canopy, a punch of floral aroma blossoming with their appearance. The trees towered over the fence and whispering at her to come explore. The fog revealed dense shrubbery and thriving plant life closer to the ground, an emerald carpet rolled out upon the sod. A stream bubbled happily through the trees, its banks rich with strange, wild bushes and ferns. So thick was the rainforest that Nova could no longer see the country surrounding the fence. The air was heavy with humidity, and she could hear the calls of foreign birds echoing from the treetops. It was lush and breathtaking, the vibrancy of the green reflecting off all the plants was incomparable. Green was her favorite color, but she had never seen it look as vivid as this. Dew dropped from the leaves to the ground, forming shallow puddles and giving the effect of steady rain. Nova sucked in a deep breath, filling her lungs with the saturated tropical air.

Mr. Russell's footfalls rang across the deck, and he lowered himself beside her. When she looked up at him, he was watching her and not the rainforest.

"Do you like it?" he questioned.

"I've never seen anything so miraculous in my entire life." Her voice was full of awe. The rainforest mesmerized her. "You're the real deal. I don't know how you could make something so elaborate using just your imagination. I don't think I'll ever be able to do that with my art."

Mr. Russell pulled his hands from behind his back, revealing her sketchbook and pencil. He smiled at her in a knowing way, a glance shared from one artist to another.

"No time like the present to try. I'll leave you alone to work." She took her supplies from him, and he returned to the house, not once looking back at his painting. Nova's excitement ignited, but she was afraid too. What if it all disappeared as soon as her foot hit the dirt? What if it was a trick only existing in her mind?

What if she couldn't capture this moment in a drawing?

Rising to her feet, she took one step at a time. The rainforest stayed intact when she tentatively approached, sneaking forward so as not to scare it away. Her confidence grew as she entered the brush. The fern leaves tickled her arms and brushed against her face as if they were trying to paint her with their emerald green. She kept the stream to her right and wandered deeper into the trees.

Craning her neck, the height of the canopy made her dizzy. She spied pops of color prancing through the branches, revealing themselves to be the most fanciful birds she'd ever encountered. One bird had a hooked beak, with feathers the blue of a bottomless ocean; another she recognized as a parrot, its plumage reminiscent of a red stop sign, begging her to pause and look. They didn't pay her any personal attention, instead flitting through the canopy in an endless game of swoops and dives. Nova was enthralled at how alive and real they seemed. Had she not known better, she would think someone had plucked her up and dropped her straight into the Amazon.

An enormous brown moth floated leisurely across the lively stream, alighting on a giant yellow flower with long tendrils of orange on the bank. Nova hunkered down in between the expansive roots of a gigantic tree, a seat of nature's own design. Flipping open her sketchbook, she pushed her hair behind her ears and started to draw. She tried to move quickly, but carefully, hoping the moth would stay put. It must have heard her telepathically, because it became still as a statue, wings aloft and shimmery in the heavy, humid air.

Nova lost all track of time and committed herself to the process. Her eyes darted to and fro, from the moth to the paper and back again. Her hand felt that familiar pull and she let it guide her. The shape of the moth was visualized in her sketchbook, and her focus was so great she didn't even need to erase. Nova was captivated by the drawing and didn't notice a sloth, its marble eyes studying her movements inquisitively, scooting next to her from higher up in the canopy.

When the creature was close enough to touch, her concentration broke. Her mouth formed a little "O" of surprise as the sloth blinked at her, its dark eyes intelligent and pensive. Tenderly, she reached out her fingertips to stroke its back. The fur was coarse and stringy as the bristles on a broom, boasting a woodsy brown sheen tinged with green to provide camouflage from predators. The sloth had claws instead of fingers, and gripped the tree easily, never once looking away from her.

Nova retracted her hand and gave the sloth some space.

"Thank you," she whispered happily. Adding the few final details to her drawing, the sloth kept her company until she finished. Nova wanted to pinch herself to prove she was awake.

The gurgling of the stream was hypnotic, and the hum of the insects acted as nature's lullaby, making her eyelids beg for a nap. She signed her name at the bottom of the picture just as the moth decided to take flight, disappearing into the trees like a phantom. Nova ran her hand over the paper, satisfied with the image she'd created. She'd captured the volume of the moth's wings and its spindly legs. The petals of the flower had been challenging in their shape, but she compared the picture to the real thing and deemed it close enough. No one would ever believe she had really seen the inspiration for this drawing. Mr. Russell had revealed the world to her through his canvas.

17 de Junio de 2012

Dearest James, my sweet Van Gogh,

Do you remember our first day in the park, when I was watching you paint, and you were watching me read? Up until that moment, I'd been a wallflower, gazing at the world through my fishbowl, observing life move, but always from the sidelines or in the pages of a book. You opened my mind to the possibilities, and I'm so grateful you struck up a conversation. I'm even flattered I was the subject of your painting that day, when initially, it unnerved me to no end.

Our life together has been easy, though not always smooth. I had thought not being able to have a child would break us, but it actually made us stronger. Your gentle understanding was what I needed to survive. Infertility was the hardest instance of my life, up until that point. I never thought about fostering and adoption as a path for us until you suggested it. Though it took me a while to warm up to the idea, and the years have flown trying to get approved, I'm happy we made the big decision together.

I want you to know that no matter what happens to me, you deserve the happiness of raising a child. We've worked at it for so long and I don't want you to give up now, regardless of if we're together. The last three years have left me tired, mentally, emotionally, and physically. I know they have also depleted you. We have to continue being honest to prepare for the future. The doctors have tried all they can, and I'm not getting better. This experience has brought my family back to me, in the most backward way possible. Between you and my mother,

I've been pampered through this pain. You both are the only reason I've managed to be so strong.

I know Amigo was brought into our family to provide me comfort, but he will do the same for you in the coming years. He was such a mischievous ball of fluff the day you brought him home. He's a good example of how our bodies do not define us. He sees and understands my needs better than those with actual sight. Keep him close and allow him to watch out for you in his way. Though my family is separated from you by distance, they too will hold you in their hearts and open their home to you should you ever need a change.

You have a tendency to withdraw when life gets challenging. You find a quiet place in your brain and hole up until the sunshine returns. That's the artist in you, and it makes me love you all the more. We have built so much together and the last thing I want is for you to vanish from your own life. I remember how it felt to be removed in that way, alive but just existing. If you can't find the strength and hope to persevere for yourself, do it for me. Remember, I am beside you every step of the way, like the playful wind rushing past or the heat of the sun on your skin.

Let yourself love and live. Promise me. I need to know you will go on, persevere, and forever remember that my heart and soul belong to you. I have seen the real you, and you are a masterpiece of a human. Go change someone else's life for the better. Love them as I would have.

Forever Yours,
Mariposa

Chapter Thirty-Six

Prisoner

After signing her drawing, Nova tucked the sketchbook away under her arm. She took her time maneuvering through the forest, soaking in the sights and sounds of her personal dream world. The sun splattered through the trees like a golden rainbow, catching the colorful plants and spotlighting their beauty. Strange bird calls rang through the canopy, and rustling could be heard through the leaves to suggest other wildlife going about its day. Though the inhabitants of the rainforest were a mystery, Nova was not afraid. Surprisingly, she felt complete trust in Mr. Russell. He had made this place and wouldn't have put anything scary in it.

Knowing the rainforest would dissipate within a day encouraged her to take her time exploring. Nova's leisurely pace was peaceful, and she delighted at every new discovery: a crystal-clear waterfall tucked into a small hill, supple hanging vines she could monkey around on, a tree full of fresh bananas ripe for the picking, and a school of exotic fish zipping through the ice cold stream. The sunlight was shrinking, and she still hadn't seen everything. The plants were so thick she could no longer spot the house as she twisted around, having lost her sense of direction.

When at last she emerged from the trees, she was adjacent to the porch. She expected to find Mr. Russell and just about jumped ten feet in the air when she noticed someone different gaping at the painted rainforest.

"Mac! What? How? You scared me to death!" Nova strode over to him and poked him imploringly in the ribs. The boy's eyes were glassy in the sparse sunlight, starstruck by the vision of the forest. He shook his head to clear it and faced her.

"I feel like I must be dead. A rainforest in Ettenborough," he gestured to the landscape, "is completely and totally bonkers!"

"This from the kid who helped me catch a leprechaun." Nova beamed at him and gave him a playful shove. Mac finally cracked a toothy smile.

"I guess I didn't realize how powerful the easel was. It conjured an entire world!" He raised his hands above his head and shouted, exhilarated, into the depths of the forest. "MAGIC IS REAL!" A toucan erupted from the canopy in fright and flapped past them, dropping an icky, white splotch near Mac's shoe. He didn't even flinch.

Nova giggled. "Turns out the easel is only a piece of the puzzle. You need an artist's heart to make it work."

She smiled at him. "Imagination is the key to creating all this... how'd you get in here anyway?"

Mac flicked a vine on the outskirts of the jungle, testing that it wasn't just a hologram.

"I knocked on the door. Mr. Russell let me in. He told me to wait for you on the deck; it was torture not bein' able to explore. I guess he wanted you to have some alone time. Do you think we can check it out now?"

Nova scrunched her nose and avoided his gaze, the daylight practically vanished as the seconds ticked by.

"It's getting too dark. It's really easy to get lost in there. Maybe Mr. Russell will paint another picture for us tomorrow." Mac's face fell in disappointment. He flopped in the grass with a defiant thump.

"Well, I wanna see it disappear then. I'll just keep waitin' here."

Nova grunted and impatiently sighed, "That could take all night! Why don't I show you the drawing I made?" She held up her sketchbook in an attempt to cheer him up.

Mac looked past her, cocking his head, toward the base of the deck. From his vantage point, he could peer underneath it. Like a zombie, he raised an arm and pointed, his eyes exaggerated orbs reflecting the dying sun. Nova crouched beside him and followed his line of sight.

She could see below the deck, and in the dim light of evening was instantly intrigued by a set of metal doors implanted into the ground. The house did not have a basement, but apparently there was a cellar with an exterior access. Peering around for Mr. Russell or Amigo the whistleblower, she pondered the curious urge in the pit of her stomach and took a step toward the cellar before chickening out. The rainforest was a special gift just for her. Best not to sour it by overstepping her bounds and entering the cellar. She shrugged and started for the wooden deck steps, trying to lure her overeager friend away from temptation. Mac, however, was raring to go exploring, all jittery and shaky like he'd drank a pot of coffee.

"Oh, come on! Just a peek! Aren't you curious about what could be down there? Maybe there's a magic wheelbarrow or somethin'."

"That's just silly..." Nova started, but paused. Her anxiety spiked when she considered the cellar could hold another mystery: Mr. Russell may be hiding something else. What harm was there in just taking a look? Certainly, the easel was the biggest secret Mr. Russell had. The contents of the cellar would be perfectly ordinary, no doubt, but her worry pushed her to find definitive proof. Nova's entire body tingled as Mac's excitement turned contagious. Nova stowed her sketchbook safely on the deck, and they ducked simultaneously, army crawling to the cellar door.

Feeling brazen, Nova grabbed the metal handles and pulled hard, expecting it to be dense and burdensome to move. She was wrong, and the door swung up and opened easily. She had to overcompensate and Mac rushed to her aid, their knuckles white and strained to keep the door from clanging against the ground. The steps leading down were smooth gray concrete, and the air coming up from the cellar smelled earthy but dry. The darkness was inky and shadowy, and she couldn't discern what lay at the bottom of the steps.

She and Mac shared an inquisitive look, and he raised his eyebrows at her as if to say "ladies first". Nova's heartbeat thumped in her eardrums as she descended into the blackness of the cellar. Instinctively, she used her hands to guide her way, feeling along the cement walls, praying she wouldn't drop feet first into the nothingness. A niggling voice in the back of her mind chided her that curiosity hadn't served her well in the past. Consumed by her need to know the residual secrets, she squelched the thought. Every time she gained access to a new part of this house another mystery sprung up in its place. Nova was desperate to know the whole, elaborate truth.

Her foot connected with a differently textured surface than the steps, perhaps packed dirt. She bounced on the balls of her feet to test the sturdiness of the floor. She had reached the bottom. Nova gazed up the stairs, feeling she had traversed an expansive tunnel. Mac was descending at a snail's pace behind her, pivoting his head about as the darkness disconcerted him. She rolled her eyes at his drama and reminded herself that she could exit at any time to keep from becoming claustrophobic.

The cellar was pitch black and spacious. Nova

couldn't pick out any details about its interior. The room was completely noiseless, absent of even a pin drop, and she squinted in every direction, trying to adjust her eyes. Ever so slowly, shapes materialized out of the shadows, but only barely. Nova reached for a pull string, hoping the cellar had electricity available. The air above her head was empty. Moving her hand back to the wall, she ran it along the cool cement until she happened on a rectangular box. A light switch! Gathering her courage, she flicked it on, and the space was flooded with artificial light. Nova's heart caught. Hundreds of eyes stared them down. She and Mac gasped in unison.

A staggering number of canvases were littered across metal storage racks, outfitted securely to the walls. The paintings were of all different sizes and shapes, but the subject of them was the same: a wild, fiery middle-aged woman. Her brown, almond-shaped eyes were ablaze with passion, as if she was ready for confrontation. Her hazelnut skin had a healthy, supple glow, and long, wavy raven locks of hair fell past her shoulders. Her lips were ruby colored and coy, like she was teasing someone in a friendly way. Her nose was dainty and well-placed on her face. Nova thought she may be the most dazzling woman she had ever seen; or at least, that's what the paintings portrayed. The canvases captured her in a variety of poses and angles and told Nova a story about her personality. She was a woman of dignity and confidence, who commanded her life in the way she held herself with poise and determination. She would not back down from a fight, but there was kindness, too, in her eyes. Through the paintings, it was as if the woman was also reading Nova's intention and personality, like she could see into her soul. She suddenly felt ridiculously self-conscious.

She approached the nearest canvas as Mac dropped to the dirt floor with a hop, his heavy thump startling her. Hand over her heart, she pursed her lips at him, and his goofy grin returned.

Stepping closer to the collection, Nova spied an inscription at the bottom corner of a canvas, tiny text that must have been painted on with the smallest of brushes. There was a date, relatively unreadable, and then a word. She leaned close, narrowing her eyes and trying to decipher it in the limited light.

"Mariposa," she breathed. "His wife."

This was the author of the letters she had liberated in the Sunshine Room. This was the woman who had been speaking to her indirectly for the last few weeks.

"Pleased to meet you," Nova whispered reverently.

She half expected the painting to wink or giggle in response, so playful were the features of the woman, but it did not move. Nova's thoughts, on the other hand, were racing.

"Whelp, this is the creepiest museum I've ever seen," Mac announced, stuffing his hands in his pockets and swiveling on the spot, absorbing it all with an incredulous expression.

"Creepy? I think she's stunning," Nova said matter-of-factly.

"I'm not talking about her." Mac jerked his thumb toward the cellar steps, gesturing to the house. "Why's he got all these down here? Seems a little weird to me. You know, weirder than a magic easel and all that."

It was strange, but Nova didn't want to doubt Mr. Russell. She'd grown fond of him. She tried to ignore Mac, refocusing on the painting.

"You're the reason he's so sad, aren't you?" she asked Mariposa, brushing her fingers across the canvas imploringly. "And when you died, he was all alone." Nova knew what it was like to lose a loved one. Emily left a huge hole in her heart when they were separated. But she couldn't understand why Mr. Russell had never talked about Mariposa, especially when Nova had been so open about her own tragic past. Mr. Russell seemed trustworthy, and now the cellar had brought his honesty back into question.

"Who paints hundreds of pictures of the same person, only to hide them away?" Mac whispered in Nova's ear, channeling his inner ghost.

"You're crazy. He probably just misses his wife," Nova insisted, but she wasn't so sure.

Mr. Russell's collection was bizarre, and more than a little off-putting, especially since he refused to talk about Mariposa. She had to give Mac that. The possible reasons for his obsession manifested in her brain, each more dubious than the last, and her heart ached with the jarring uncertainty. The trickle of doubt turned into a flood, and she fought to paddle through it.

"Should I ask him why he locked you away? What would you have done?" She got even with Mariposa's face, nose to nose, beseeching her. Mariposa was a free spirit, both stubborn and outspoken. Nova bolstered herself with painted bravery, filling herself up like an empty cup.

"There's only one way to find out. Come on." Nova commanded, grabbing Mac by the sleeve.

Casting one final glance backward, she turned off the light with a swat and ascended the steps, a war being waged inside of her. The thought of losing Mr. Russell placed a tremendous knot in her throat and debilitating tension in her shoulders. She had to find the truth, no matter the cost.

Chapter Thirty-Seven

Mariposa

Mac graciously excused himself once they were back on the deck, hesitating solemnly before he left; he seemed worried when he questioned if she would be okay. Nova sloughed off his concern and waved him away, promising he could come back tomorrow for a new painting adventure. Her palms were sweaty as she watched him disappear into the house like a spirit into the night.

Mr. Russell joined her shortly thereafter. They ate dinner on the deck in the open air, and Mr. Russell was in chatterbox mode. Though sounds from the rainforest punctuated the background noise, Nova tried her best to focus on the conversation. Mariposa's face was running on a loop through her brain.

"If you like, we can have a set time every week to paint. It's been forever since I learned basic technique, but I could give you a few pointers as you practice." Mr. Russell took a big bite of PB&J, gesturing to the tropical landscape of the backyard. "I would love to see your drawing. Did you enjoy your time in the painting?"

Nova mustered a smile. "Mmmmm-hmmmm. It was incredible." She took a bite of her sandwich to fill the silence, chewing as slow and inconspicuously as she could.

"We had a forest behind our house as children. That's where my grandfather taught me to paint, so trees are second nature to me. You should have seen me traipsing around the woods in a cast. I was not very graceful." Mr. Russell's sentences strung together excitedly, like a child lacing beads in quick succession. Nova couldn't bring herself to break his mood. She sat quietly and listened, all the while picturing Mariposa and her stubborn eyes. Maybe Nova didn't have the gumption it would take to confront him.

"Are you feeling alright?" Mr. Russell stopped talking, noticing the concern wreaking havoc on her face. His response was so genuine, so worried, Nova almost spilled her guts and confessed. Almost.

"I'm just a little nauseous. I think it was the heat from being in the rainforest. If it's okay, I may go upstairs to rest. I'm not really hungry."

"Let me know if you need anything." Mr. Russell interjected, confused, as she rushed into the house.

Nova placed her dish in the sink as she passed and

took the stairs two at a time, panicking. She couldn't remember the last time a decision this big was put on her shoulders. Her anxiety skyrocketed, even in the Sunshine Room, and she paced hysterically about. The moon rose into the sky like a foreboding interrogation lamp. She couldn't shake the feeling that her latest discovery made her position in this house precarious and temporary. When she stayed with Emily, she had inadvertently caused her own departure. Her art had prompted Emily's parents to send her away. Against her better judgment, she entertained building a life here with Mr. Russell. Would confronting him destroy her chance? Could she even make a home here if he was keeping such enormous secrets? He loved Mariposa well enough to paint her, but had never once mentioned her name. Not. Once.

Nova splayed across the bed and covered her face with a pillow, wanting to scream. She lay like that for a long time, dragging her breath in and out, willing her heart to slow and her indecision to clear. The room was completely dark now, swallowed by pitch black nighttime. After much deliberation, Nova made up her mind.

She had a right to know.

Striding immediately to the armoire, she retrieved the dainty key from its hiding place. Before she lost her nerve, she speedily unlocked the end table; the familiar whiff of flowers ascended from the drawer as she slid it open. *The perfume belonged to her,* Nova realized in an instant.

Nova pulled the letters out with great care, feeling responsible now that she had met Mariposa in the cellar. She'd read all but one of the letters. The final envelope was sealed, and she hadn't had the courage to rip it open. Strangely enough, it was not labeled with a number. Instead, the envelope read "James" in a neat, winding script.

Dakota leapt to the top of the end table, mewing at Nova for attention. Nova scratched the calico's chin and gazed forlornly into her gemlike eyes.

"I don't know what's going to happen, but no matter what, you'll never be homeless again. I'll make sure of that," she whispered reassuringly, half to Dakota, half to herself. It was time to take control of her own destiny—come what may.

Straightening herself and adjusting her face into a resolute expression, she exited the Sunshine Room, letters cradled in her arms. The attic light shone down the hall, and Nova climbed the stairs as slowly as the sloth, forcing her feet to keep going up, up, up.

Mr. Russell was tidying the easel, humming a tune while he worked with his back to the staircase. Nova was filled with regret, knowing her questions could create a rift between them, but something in her soul had cracked, and she could no longer sit idle. She'd spent her entire life without a voice or a choice. At least this way, she could finally speak.

Nova cleared her throat.

"Who is Mariposa?" She knew the answer already, but wanted to hear him admit it.

It took Mr. Russell a moment to register, and he was still smiling as he turned around.

"What's that?" he asked her, caught up in a blissful daydream.

"Who is Mariposa?"

Nova stepped forward and set the stack of letters on his stool. Mr. Russell was a statue, all except his face. First, he was surprised, his mouth ajar, and then his visage fell into a dark hole. Defeat played about his features, dragging him down like quicksand, as his hand hovered over the envelopes, palm trembling but not quite touching the paper.

Mr. Russell fought to control his emotions. His eyes were two deep pools of pain, and he couldn't tear them away from the letters, not even for a second. A tear rolled down his cheek when he finally answered.

"Mariposa means butterfly in Spanish." His voice was hushed and crackling, like embers in a dying fire.

"Who is she? What happened to her?" Nova stood firm, pushing herself onward. She needed the straight truth like she needed air to breathe.

"She's the person who taught me that the easel doesn't work for real subjects."

At long last, his hand came to rest atop the pile. The energy left him, his body visibly deflating like a punctured balloon. You could see him reaching for an anchor… something steady to hold onto.

"Where… where did you find these letters?" Mr. Russell asked.

Against her better judgment, Nova's anger rose in her chest at his avoidance of the whole truth. He had changed the subject again. A blind fury ripped through her. Her emotions were an overreaction built up over years of staying silent and feeling powerless. Why did no one believe she deserved honesty? The floodgates opened now, and she refused to back down.

"In the end table in my room. I didn't know they were important until I read them. Stop stalling. Explain the truth. Why didn't you tell me her story?" She demanded directly.

Mr. Russell was aghast. "You read all the letters?"

"Not all of them. One is still sealed." Nova indignantly responded.

Consumed by shock and quick as a jack rabbit, Mr. Russell tore through the envelopes, searching for the final letter. Nova stumbled back, startled and pale at his knee-jerk reaction.

He was shaking when he pulled the appropriate envelope from the pile, his eyes were red and brimmed with salty tears. He held the envelope to his forehead and sucked in a deep, rattling breath. The tremors shook his entire body, and he seemed as though he may collapse. Nova reached forward to brace him.

The attic exploded with bellows of pent-up rage, laced by indescribable sorrow.

"You had no right to go through my private things!" Mr. Russell shouted, his voice venomous and hurt. The sadness in his eyes consumed him, and it was as if he wasn't even seeing her anymore. Nova could only stare and blink as he seethed, the grief pouring over him like a tidal wave.

"I've tried to be understanding, I've tried to be patient!" He flung the opened letters across the floor in disgust.

Nova cringed and squeezed her eyes shut. His raw emotions caught her off guard. She stammered and tried to think of an apologetic response.

"I didn't know the letters were yours. I read them before I realized." She hated how weak she sounded, how his response counteracted the courage she'd found. Mariposa's face appeared in Nova's swimming vision, and then Emily's. Nova's heart hardened. "You have no right to keep secrets from me. Every inch of this house is covered in lies. You're keeping me in the dark on purpose."

Mr. Russell strode away from her, hiding his face, not immediately knowing what to say. Nova was tired of being the only one to feel hurt. She dug the knife in deeper, a life of loneliness getting the best of her.

"When were you going to mention the cellar and the hundreds and hundreds of paintings of Mariposa? I bet you lied to her too. How could you lie to someone you supposedly loved? And how do you expect me to trust you?" Nova's hands were fists, her body tense. She instantly regretted prodding him but couldn't return to her rational mind.

When Mr. Russell spun around, it occurred to her immediately she'd gone too far. His chest was heaving, his face drenched in tears. The look he gave her was haunting and chilled her to the bone. For the first time, she felt ashamed of the grief she'd unleashed.

"What do you know about family? You've never been a part of one," he whispered back, each syllable laced with poison. He was trembling so violently Nova couldn't believe he was still standing. She recoiled as if she'd been physically slapped.

"Go. To. Your. Room." He pointed to the stairs to emphasize. It was over.

"Gladly," she replied, outwardly fired up and inwardly reeling, stomping down the stairs as she went. Nova slammed the door to the Sunshine Room so hard the furniture shook. Dakota yowled and hid under the bed.

She hadn't known Mr. Russell could be so spiteful and angry, and hadn't realized the extreme depths of his sorrow. The sympathy she'd had for him was extinguished by how helpless he made her feel. Once again, she was alone and vulnerable, stranded on an island of someone else's bidding. She swore she'd never give anyone the chance to abandon her again. It was now or never. Nova looked desperately around the room, fearing her time to escape was running low. She was a fool for thinking this house would be any different than the others, and she chastised herself for not leaving earlier in search of her real home. She wouldn't miss this opportunity.

A gentle knock resounded from the door, timid and apologetic. Mr. Russell had come to make amends. Nova held back a sob as he spoke through the door.

"I didn't mean... I'm awfully sorry... I shouldn't have yelled or said those terrible things." His sentiments were jumbled and random, like he couldn't pronounce the words right. As if they'd been extracted from the bottom of a bottle. Nova physically ached at the regret in his voice, but a door in her heart had also slammed shut. She would not be hurt again.

"Just leave me alone!" She screamed, chucking her pillow at the door with a muted thud. The silence between them was so thick she could have ladled it like soup. At last, she heard him retreat down the hallway in defeat, and she could sense the rift between them growing with each step. It was torture, plain and simple.

The front door clanged and drew her attention to the window. Mr. Russell's darkened silhouette was moving toward the garage. He had an envelope in one hand and a bottle in the other. Amigo trailed after him protectively. The truck engine came alive, and he drove away down the road, heading in the direction of the pond. Amigo accompanied him, sitting somberly in the bed of the truck. This was her chance, and she was going to take it, but she had some business to attend to first.

Chapter Thirty-Eight

Revenge

Wrenching open her door, she hurtled into the hall and back to the attic. Nova was so worked up that the positive atmosphere of the space had dissipated, leaving her feeling like a void black hole. Her intention had been to retrieve a keepsake, but seeing the scattered letters caused her to pause. The slow burning fire of hurt reignited in her belly, and she decided to spare a few more minutes.

It may have been immature, it may have been cruel, but a juvenile piece of Nova was finished being pushed around, tired of being emotionally hung out to dry and abandoned. Seeing Emily's parents in her mind's eye, revenge took root, and she hunted the house for a metal bin of some kind... a small trash can perhaps. She had to make do with an empty paint can. Rifling through the kitchen drawers, she located a book of matches and then charged up the stairs, all the way to the third floor. She placed the paint can ceremoniously into the middle of the room, a centerpiece of her own making. Gathering the discarded letters, she mentally apologized to Mariposa as she stuffed them into the paint can. The lonely toddler, lost child, and wayward soul living in her broken heart begged to be avenged. All the families who had wronged her stared back through the paint can, like it was a portal to her most desolate memories. Years of being invisible culminated in a terrible cacophony of emotion, and she wished to reclaim some semblance of personal strength and self-acceptance. Burning the letters would mean she could never come back here, but it had to be done. She needed him to see the ashes after she'd left, to know she was in control of her own destiny... that she was done being pushed passively away.

Planting her feet in front of the paint can, Nova pulled a solitary match from the package. She held it up before her face, marveling at the resemblance it bore in shape to a paintbrush. The tiny handle was made of wood, and instead of a brush, the match had a cherry red bulb at the end. Its purpose was the opposite of art. Brushes were for creating; fire would only obliterate.

Nova scraped the match across the sandpaper surface of the matchbook, and a lively flame sprang forth. It danced entrancingly before her eyes; she could feel the heat of it on her fingertips and the tip of her nose. She held out her arm above the paint can, mentally counting backward from ten, digging deep within for a power she had never had, to reclaim her sense of self-worth. At the last second, she made eye contact with the letters. Mariposa's name stared back at her, and in an instant, her face was there too. Her mouth was set in a little frown, and her eyes were sad and remorseful. She gave Nova a small nod, as if to say she could do what she needed to. Mariposa forgave her. Nova wailed in frustration, and promptly blew out the match.

She couldn't erase Mariposa. She couldn't be responsible for someone being forgotten. She knew too well how it felt to be forgotten.

Nova couldn't bring herself to destroy the letters.

She screamed angrily, tears rolling openly down her cheeks, and dropped the extinguished, smoking match into the paint can. She wanted to spare Mariposa but decided to leave the evidence for Mr. Russell to find. That way he'd know what she could have done, if she'd really wanted to. A piece of Nova felt relieved she hadn't followed through. Mr. Russell's grief was burned into her retinas; when she closed her eyes, she could see his pain. Nothing good could come from pain. Remembering her original inspiration, Nova solemnly accessed the secret panel in the side cabinet, withdrawing the hand carved paintbrush from its nook. It would be the last keepsake she'd ever claim. Despite herself, guilt gnawed at her stomach for swiping it. Old habits die hard.

Chapter Thirty-Nine

Trapped

The next ten minutes were a frenzy of planning and packing. Nova shut her bedroom door and set herself to the task of gathering her treasures into her denim backpack. She almost left the sketchbook on the end table but decided it would be a waste of perfectly good paper. It just barely fit. She tucked each item intentionally into place, saving the paintbrush for last. It sat at the top of the pile like a bow on a present. Dakota watched her actions morosely, as if she could sense change coming. Her tiny tail twitched back and forth.

Nova donned her favorite sweatshirt but left all of her other clothes in the armoire. She didn't want any more reminders of this place. This was the first moment the Sunshine Room left her feeling cold inside. She shivered as she observed it for the final time. Something instinctual, a gentle tug, told her Mariposa was responsible for its beauty. She muttered a quick "Thank you" as she zipped up her backpack. Nova still needed to prepare for the cross-country road trip. She would have to snatch some food and water from the kitchen. Dakota meowed dismally, and Nova remembered that cat food was essential too. She didn't know how she would convince Emily's parents to let Dakota stay, but she had to try. She'd made the kitten a promise.

Full of unease, Nova trod over to Dakota and plucked the little furball up off the ground. She nuzzled her on the cheek and cuddled her in the folds of her sweatshirt, saying a silent prayer that they would make it to their faraway destination unscathed. Dakota, usually somewhat affectionate, was stiff and bristly. The kitten jerked and pulled to escape from Nova's hands, sniffing at the air and skittishly peering about. A stone settled in the pit of Nova's stomach. Perhaps Dakota was anxious about the journey too.

It wasn't until she opened the bedroom door that she realized something had gone disastrously wrong. A dark, viscous smoke filled the hallway, plumes of it rushing into the Sunshine Room as the door swung open. An imposing heat tumbled into the space and Nova felt panic deep in her bones as she glanced, horrified, toward the attic. A faint crackling could be heard as the smoke swelled down the staircase, sparks catching on the stairs and igniting into blooms of fire.

Somehow, to her absolute horror, the match had lit the letters. So quickly were the flames advancing that they had already progressed down the staircase, blocking the hall.

Hacking and coughing, Nova retreated to the Sunshine Room, shutting the door and sinking to the ground, stymied at the turn of events. The smoke stung her eyes and confused her lungs. *DANGER, DANGER, DANGER* rang like an alarm bell in her head. Dakota was panicking too, scrambling across the floor toward the window.

The window! Nova shouldered her backpack and rushed across the room. Unlatching the window, she pushed upward with all her might. It didn't budge. She pushed again, with more effort, bracing her shoulder against the frame and scraping the palms of her hands until they were raw. It was no use. The window would not open. Running her finger along the trim, Nova could feel the smooth surface of nails pounded into the wood. She collapsed in surprise. Mr. Russell had hammered the windows shut, presumably after her first escape attempt. She whimpered in frustration and fear. The glow of fire danced underneath the door frame and smoke was sneaking into the room through the same cracks. She didn't have much time.

Tossing up her hood, she spoke softly to Dakota, trying to calm her. Nova stroked the kitten and dropped her down into her sweatshirt, remembering the night she carried her home the same way. The word brought a stinging pain. Home.

Trying to think clearly in spite of the rising temperature and the murky smoke, Nova pounded and kicked at the glass of the window. She needed to find a way to break it; she wasn't strong enough on her own. Frantically, she examined the room for a piece of furniture small enough to hoist. Outside of a lamp on the end table, she was out of luck.

In a last-ditch effort, she seized the lamp and swung it with all her might. The smoke was so thick she had to guess the location of the window, but she heard a satisfying crash. Glass rained down upon the floor and Nova shielded her face from the debris.

Discouragingly, upon further inspection, the window remained intact, a tiny sliver of a crack visible upon its surface. The breaking glass had come from the bulb of the lamp. Nova beat at the glass barrier, screaming as loudly as she could for help. The terror was debilitating, and with every second that passed, the less she could breathe. Her energy was diminishing quickly. She didn't want to die.

Slinging her arms around her belly to shelter Dakota, Nova sank to the floor, trying to avoid the smoke. The room was almost full now, and her head felt foggy. She wheezed as she curled into a fetal position, stroking Dakota with a single finger, trying to reassure her. The kitten licked at Nova's finger with her sandpaper tongue. Nova wrapped her body into a tight, miniscule ball, determined to protect Dakota. The fear had turned to numbness, and a tear trickled down her cheek. She gasped and hacked, aching for air.

The crackling transformed into a thunderous roar as the fire made a valiant effort to breach the Sunshine Room. It wouldn't be long now. Feeling groggy, Nova closed her eyes. She expected to see Emily, or even Mariposa, visiting her for the last time. To her surprise, her mind's eye conjured up Mr. Russell, but not the recent angry Mr. Russell. She pictured Mr. Russell as he had been when he'd taken care of her, with his sad eyes and his genuine smile.

"I'm sorry," she whispered, and she meant it.

The popping of the flames outside the door grew in volume, drowning out even her thoughts. Teetering on the edge of consciousness, Nova heard a faint noise from outside. An animal of some kind, panic-stricken from the fire. Was that... barking?

Chapter Forty

Cocoon

Nova fought to stay conscious, straining to hear if help was on the way. There was definitely barking coming from outside; loud woofs that gave her something to focus on other than the smoke. From beyond the window, she heard a sudden thud, like a tree branch landing on the roof. Not long after, footsteps could be discerned approaching the window.

Nova weakly tried to get to her feet, calling out in a scratchy voice for help. There were small taps reverberating from the window, a flicker of hope. She sobbed in relief. Grasping the sill with both hands, she pulled herself up with her remaining strength.

Nose pushed up against the glass, she could just make out a familiar face staring back at her, though it swam before her in double vision like a hallucination. Mr. Russell had returned, and he looked petrified. His teeth were clenched, and his mouth set in a grim slash. Motioning her away from the window, he stepped back from the glass and raised his hands. Nova jolted toward the bed, falling out of the way.

A sledgehammer connected with the window, the barrier disintegrating instantaneously to dust. Glass showered through the air and Nova ducked under the bed clumsily, trying to avoid the spray. Already, the smoke was pouring through the broken window, emptying out into the night as a rushing graphite river. The room cleared just the slightest bit.

Mr. Russell used the handle of the sledgehammer to break the jagged pieces of glass from the window frame, and then clambered through. Nova couldn't speak but held out her hand to him. He leaned down and took her up in his arms, balancing her weight against his chest. She sank into him, relief coursing through her veins, balanced between conscious and unconscious like a top about to fall.

The door to the Sunshine Room made an ungodly noise as the fibers of wood cracked and contorted from the heat. Mr. Russell hastened to the window, helping Nova crawl through the gap first. She scooted out onto the roof, getting déjà vu of her initial night of escape. The storm had howled and threatened to knock her over then. She took a moment to lay back and be still as Mr. Russell made his way onto the roof. Dakota stuck an ear out the top of her sweatshirt, swiveling it back and forth, listening for danger. Tonight, the stars were clear and bright, beaming through the discarded smoke, twinkling enticingly. She let the fresh country air seep into her lungs in a long, drawn-out breath. She was alive.

Mr. Russell lifted her to her feet and guided her toward the edge of the roof. A ladder was braced against the shingles. Shakily, Nova lowered herself onto the rungs. From outside, the entire house was a giant, makeshift chimney. Colossal columns of smoke rose into the sky like a dark flag of surrender. Nova gasped when she spied the attic window. The visible wood was blackened and scarred, and the flames reached like despicable arms from the depths of the room. Naively, she hesitated.

"The easel!" Nova coughed.

She went to climb back up the ladder to get to the attic, but Mr. Russell stopped her.

"It's gone," he insisted.

Nova's heart plummeted in grief. She grabbed the ladder for support and started to cry. One step at a time, she moved toward the grass and salvation. She couldn't rip her eyes away from the attic, wishing she hadn't been so stupid and rash.

When they'd made it to the ground, Mr. Russell ushered her across the road to take refuge by the apple trees. Amigo galloped in circles around them, yipping happily and herding them away from the house. Nova was beside herself. Once they'd created distance from the inferno, she collapsed, heartbroken, sobbing into her hands.

"I'm... I'm... so... sorry." Her voice was broken and

sorrowful, her guarded exterior completely shattered. She couldn't stop crying; she became pure tears.

Mr. Russell stretched his arms around her, nestling her into a cocoon of safety and love, and responded.

"I'm not. You're safe. That's all that matters."

They stayed like that while the fire surged, decimating the upper floors of the house. The chalky moon watched as a sentry over the horizon. Nova gave herself into the darkness, desperate for forgiveness and grateful for Mr. Russell's sturdy presence. Miles away came the sound of sirens, growing ever closer.

****

Dawn arrived and the smoke dissipated. The upper floors of the house were unrecognizable, blackened by soot, a hideous stain against the sapphire morning sky. Someone had given Nova a wool blanket in the night, and she wrapped it around her head like a cloak, protecting her from the nightmare of reality. She longed to wake from this tragic mess.

The firefighters left once they confirmed the farmhouse as stable. Mr. Russell wrapped his arm around her as they approached the porch, guiding her up the steps and through the front door. Nova braced herself for the damage, but her heart had grown disturbingly numb from the loss of the easel. The entranceway and kitchen appeared normal, but upon reaching the banister for the stairs, the skeleton of the house reared its ugly head. The once beautiful wooden stairs were cracked, warped, and charred, leading into a pit of darkness and ruin. Ash turned the upper floors into a ghost town, the walls a ghastly gray where they weren't burned black. Nova covered her eyes and backed away from the horrific scene, her breathing shallow and ragged. She hit the kitchen wall with her back and plopped to the floor, covering her head completely with the blanket, summoning a few meager tears to empty herself out. Dakota and Amigo stayed loyally on the porch, not wanting to come inside.

Mr. Russell sat cautiously beside her, his arm hovering above the blanket before again holding onto her shoulders. His voice was quiet, but peaceful, as he tried to reach her through the loss.

"We can take a few things with us to Ms. Ellie's to tide us over while the house is repaired. Is there anything you need?"

Nova dropped the blanket to reveal that she was still wearing her backpack, unable to meet Mr. Russell in the eyes. She whispered in response, fractured.

"I wish I could go back in time to save the magic. I never meant for any of this to happen..." She buried her head in his chest, struck by a comforting smell of paint and something else... something new. Familiarity? Security? Home? Home.

"I'm ready for a new chapter after all these years." He hugged her then, and she let him. The moment was medicine to the illness of her soul. Something told her Mr. Russell knew how to mend a broken heart. He had much to teach her in the days to come.

Groaning as he stood, his joints popping, Mr. Russell held out both hands to help her up. She took his calloused fingers without an ounce of hesitation and forgot the blanket on the ground in a lumpy heap. Some baggage was better left behind.

"Will you be a part of my story?" Mr. Russell smiled as he said it, but she could see the doubt in his eyes. He waited patiently for her reply. Nova took his hand in hers with a squeeze and smiled back.

"Yes."

A playful breeze accompanied them out of the house and into the sunshine.

July 7th
Dear Emily,

I want to begin by apologizing. I regret the way I said goodbye. I hope you can forgive me for getting so angry. You were, and always will be, my best friend. A lot has happened since I left, and I feel like a new person, but in a good way.

Mr. Briar said he would be sure to hand deliver this letter to you. My new guardian, Mr. Russell, suggested that I write as a way to keep in touch. I'm hoping once you see my letter, you'll be able to send one back. I'm living in a town called Ettenborough. It's the smallest town ever, and I wasn't impressed when I first got to Mr. Russell's house. The people have been kind to me though. And cross my heart, you'll never guess what I found: real-life magic.

About a month ago, I made a huge mistake. I accidentally started a house fire that caused a ton of damage. I got really lucky, though. Mr. Russell was close by, saw the smoke, and saved me. He lost something magical that was very precious to him. I will always feel responsible. We celebrated Mr. Russell's birthday this week, and I gave him a keepsake I smuggled from the house... a special paintbrush that may help me make amends with him. When he opened the gift wrap, the paintbrush started glowing bright, like a baby firefly. Mr. Russell thinks maybe the magic hasn't abandoned us after all. Once we're done with the renovations, he promised we'll test the paintbrush and see what it does. The paintbrush's shimmer shines brightest when we're together. I think it knows we're supposed to be a family. I still haven't forgiven myself for my past mistakes. Every day, I get a little closer though, kind of like a half-finished painting.

I met a boy named Mac and he's an artist too. You'd like him, he's funny and brave and acted as a friend even before I was nice to him. I found out he's in my class this fall, so I'm guessing there are some adventures waiting for me when I start school. Ms. Ellie works at the diner in town, and she stops by to visit on her days off. You can tell she cares about me and Mr. Russell. She's letting us live with her while we fix the house, which is very generous with the animals we bring along. Amigo and Dakota are our pets, a dog and a kitten, and they're practically siblings, the way they follow each other around. They're different, but alike enough they love each other all the same.

I've learned Mr. Russell lost his wife to illness, a headstrong, loving woman named Mariposa. She was an insanely talented carpenter; she could build almost anything! Mr. Russell talks about her as we work on repairing the farmhouse. It took him a long time to open up, but now he laughs when he says her name. She got sick and passed away over five years ago. He loved her more than he loves anything else, and though she's gone, I can feel her with us in the house. Sometimes I think she could be the breeze or my Sunshine Room or even the place where magic comes from. Does that sound crazy?

Mr. Russell painted a hundred pictures of her and hid them all away. I had the idea we should hang one of the paintings in the new attic, and he spent an entire day picking out which portrait to use. The one he picked is lovely. It makes me happy to see him smiling at the portrait.

He promises he's going to teach me more about art. I told him about the way you introduced me to it, and I cherish the art I've created because of you. It kept me believing life could be better. Thank you for giving me my hope.

It won't always be easy, but I'm ready to paint my own life. I want to have a home and allow myself to be happy. I promised myself I would make it back to you, but I see now that this is where I belong. I need Mr. Russell and he needs me. As a wise man once said, "There is nothing more truly artistic than to love people".

Friends forever,
Nova Russell

Acknowledgments

They say it takes a village to raise a child, and Nova is no exception to this rule. I am a great reader of books, but I never fathomed the amount of effort and connections it would take to "raise one". I let Nova's story percolate in my mind for fifteen years before finding the courage to bring her to life on the page, and I owe that courage to all of the amazing family members and friends that have carried me down this intimidating path. There would be no story if it wasn't for all of you. So, to start, I'd like to give an enormous thank you to Tess Kane and my sister, Sarah Ann Doughty, for the gorgeous cover and interior artwork. You brought the magic of art to life.

Thank you to Dennis and Mary Doughty for being the first to welcome Nova with open arms. Much thanks to Lexi Weber, Dan Weber, Susan Kischkel, Mark Kischkel, Keith Baker, Barbara Baker, Scott Jedlicka, and Jackie Smith for loving Nova as much as I do and helping me shine a spotlight on her beautiful journey. Thank you to all of the phenomenal readers who took a chance on The Painter's Butterfly and helped polish it into the diamond it is today: Di Litwer, Rebecca McClafferty, Lawrence McClafferty (the fastest child reader I've ever had the honor to 'meet'), Nemo Lockeheart, Nathalie Laine, Christiana Doucette, Sarah Sebuchi, Kumi Sebuchi,

Kenzo Sebuchi, Sarah McKnight, Reese Guerra, Lisa Borne Graves and son, Sara Kapadia, and the amazing #MGpies and #WritingCommunity on Twitter. I owe a debt of gratitude to my fantastic friend and editor, Nichole Brazelton, for having tremendous vision and faith in my novel (and me)! And finally, a giant thank you to Keivon Liburd, the embodiment of pure kindness, for steering my submission materials in the right direction. Rest in peace, my friend.

Thank you to the fantastic team at Kinkajou Press for believing in my work and helping me share Nova's artistry with the world. An exuberant thanks to my dear friend, Elli Saathoff, without whom I never would have found the confidence to pick up a pen and begin. Your friendship is pure gold. And lastly, thank you, fellow readers, for caring enough about Nova to walk beside her as she searched for her true home. Whatever that crazy dream is that you keep hidden away inside you... pursue it now. Don't fret another minute or delay. You are capable of ANYTHING you set your mind to. I believe in you.

You don't need a magic easel to make your dreams come true. Your creative and loving spirit is enough.

Author Bio

Rebecca Weber is a Midwestern girl with a lifelong passion for books! She spends most of her time nurturing her two Boston Terrier fur-babies and flipping houses with her realtor husband. It took fifteen years to find the courage to craft her first novel, *The Painter's Butterfly*, but now she's never letting her feather pen go! While she misses teaching preschool-aged children their ABC's, Rebecca is thrilled to have the chance to reach middle graders worldwide with her fantastical stories.